Grayson's ENLIGHTENMENT

HONEY CREEK DEN BOOK 4

TAYLOR RYLAN

Jay,
Are you #teambabyalpha or #teampanda

Hugs,
Taylor Rylan

Copyright © 2018 by Taylor Rylan

Published in the United States by Taylor Rylan

All rights reserved. No part of this book may be reproduced, copied, or transmitted in any format or by any means without the prior written permission from the author.

This book is a work of fiction. Names, characters, places, and events are a product of the author's imagination. Any similarities to actual persons, living or dead, is pure coincidence. As are any similarities to any businesses, events or locations.

All products and brand names mentioned are registered trademarks of their respective holder and or company. I do not own the rights to these, nor do I claim to.

Cover Design by Jay Aheer of Simply Defined Art

Caution

This is a gay romance that contains the following:

Adult language, adult situations, explicit sexual material between two men over the age of 18. Guy parts are seriously going to be touching, knotting, and vibrating. This book is intended for **ADULTS ONLY**.

Note to Readers

I just want to first say thanks for giving my take on shifters a chance. In my world, shifters live multiple centuries and only knot and reproduce with their fated mate. Mates can be found anywhere, and you'll meet many multiple species couples in my world. I hope you enjoy Grayson and Jai's story.

And for those that have already asked…

Jai is pronounced with a long "I" (J-eye)

Bà is dad in Mandarin

Bàbà is father in Mandarin

Érzi is son in Mandarin

Li is pronounced with a long "E" (Lee)

Grayson — 1

"Grayson! Did you get the last of your stuff?"

"Yeah, Da! I'm going to be late for my first day of work if I don't get going," I shouted as I walked down the stairs with the last box of my things. Alpha War offered me a small cabin on den land and after I returned from my two-week crash course training, I started moving everything in. My alpha dad wasn't happy, but Da overruled him and said it was time for me to have the freedoms a young alpha needed. Whatever that meant.

"I can't tell you how proud I am of you. Don't worry about your dad. He'll come around soon enough," Da said as I stepped down off of the last step.

"I don't know, Da. I feel like he's upset with me for whatever reason. Like, I need to be more like him. He always seems so mad, and I don't know what to do about it."

"Grayson, your father was very young when we mated. Younger than you. His parents didn't prepare him for anything having to do with mates and what to expect or not. That all fell on me and he's stubborn. Most of the time he didn't listen. Still won't.

But you, you're a wonderful young man and alpha. You'll make some omega a perfect mate someday. I just know it. I'll always be here to answer any questions you have. If I can't answer them, and you need to talk to an alpha, I'm sure that one of the alphas in the den would answer any questions you have if your dad won't."

"Thanks, Da. Love you. But I really gotta go. Thanks for everything. I know it's caused Dad to become upset with you."

My carrier shrugged before responding. "Not the first time, won't be the last. Now, again, have a good first day at work and be sure to call or text when you get home. I know you're twenty-one now, and you're living in your own place, but I still worry."

"I know, Da. I will." I glanced at my watch and saw that it was later than I thought, and I wouldn't have time to stop at my cabin and drop off my boxes before heading into work. It was more important to be on time than it was to get back to my cabin and drop stuff off, so I climbed into my old pickup and headed to work. So much had changed in just the last few months. Until a year ago, I'd never been out of Alaska. Then suddenly we were running for our lives in the middle of the night and didn't stop until Dad thought we were finally far enough away. If nothing else, he was good at getting us out of harm's way.

I was about to start my dream job, and I didn't want to mess it up, so I prayed I didn't get caught in all of the lights in town. If I did, I'd certainly be late. If I didn't, then it'd still be close. I knew

Ryker was taking a chance on me, and I wanted to make him proud. Sure I had a dad and da, but after what happened all those years ago, as well as right after we found sanctuary here in Honey Creek, I wanted to be seen as a worthy member.

Luckily for me, I caught all of the lights green—there were only three—and I made it to the ranger station with just a few minutes to spare. Not exactly how I wanted to start my first day on the job, but it was better than being late. I'd be sure to tell Ryker that I'd be earlier tomorrow. I didn't want him to think it was a habit to show up just barely on time.

When I got out of the truck, my bear perked up and pulled me towards the building. I told him to stop and wait, but he didn't want to listen. I knew he was excited about the prospect of having a job that allowed us to spend a lot of time outside, but he was being ridiculous. When I got next to the building, I was hit with a tangy scent that had my bear begging to burst free. When I looked down at my almost instantly hard dick, my bear suddenly yelled *mate! Ours!*

I couldn't stop the loud growl that escaped my throat, and when I strode up to the door, I threw it open and zeroed in on the only person in the room I hadn't met yet. I didn't know who he was except that he smelled wonderful and he was our mate. His caramel skin, black hair, almond-shaped dark brown eyes, and slim build drew me unlike any other before. He dropped the coffee mug he'd been holding, and he just stood there staring, as if he were shocked and maybe a little scared.

Having our mate be afraid of us was the last thing my bear and I wanted. I started to move towards him when suddenly Ryker and Troy both started laughing. I gave them a quick glance but then zeroed back in on my mate. Slowly I approached, trying to appear much calmer and not scare him. He rolled his eyes and turned and looked at Ryker and then Troy. When he did, they laughed louder and he swatted at Troy, who just about fell over from laughing so hard. It was Ryker who got it together first.

"Well, I see the fates have been at it again. Shall I introduce you two? I'm sure you've figured out who you are to each other by now though."

"That won't be necessary," our mate said to Ryker before he turned back to look at me and walked the last two steps towards me and stopped directly in front of me.

He was several inches shorter than my own six-three height, but I didn't care. The top of his head only came to my chin, but my bear and I both found him gorgeous and loved the idea of having a shorter mate. He was absolutely beautiful, and he smelled like ours.

"You must be Grayson, our new ranger. Hi, I'm Jai." He thrust his hand out to me, and when I placed mine in his, I felt a tingle go through my entire body.

"Yes, I'm Grayson. It's so nice to meet you." I was at a complete loss of what to do. What did you do when you met your mate? Da hadn't ever really said anything other than when Dad found him, he left with him. Was I supposed to take Jai away with me? We were in the same den. Da and Dad weren't. And that was fifty years ago. Things were different now, right?

I looked down into Jai's dark brown eyes and saw a glimmer of mischief in them. He smiled at me, and I couldn't help but smile back.

"Jai, be nice. He's really young and trying to figure things out," Troy said to my mate. In a way, I wanted to say thank you to the older alpha, but at the same time, I wanted to rip his head off for talking to my mate like that.

"Don't worry, Troy. I have every intention of being *nice* to Grayson. I realize it's only eight in the morning, but I think it would probably be best if I take Grayson out and show him the south beach at the lake. We'll be back for the lunch you two have planned," Jai said as he walked past me, grabbing my hand as he did. I looked over to Troy and Ryker and shrugged as I turned and followed my mate out of the building I'd just rushed to get in to.

"Do you want to drive or should I? Do you have a problem with omegas driving?"

"Why would I have a problem with you driving? Haven't you been doing it for a while now? Besides, you know the area so much better than me. It'd be better if you drove."

"Thank the fates. I know you're young, and honestly, I'm a little worried. Here, hop-in." Jai opened the passenger door of his black pickup truck for me. When I climbed into the newer model, I glanced over at my beat-up truck and realized that I really wasn't ready for a mate. Nowhere near ready. I had nothing to offer. I'd just turned twenty-one recently, and I hadn't even really started my first day on my first real job yet. I had almost no savings, and yet, here I was sitting in the passenger seat of my mate's truck.

I knew he was older than me. And most likely, quite a bit older. He'd obviously had a bit more time to get his life together before we found each other. What could I really offer? Sadly I realized, absolutely nothing. I looked out the passenger window and watched the scenery go by as my mate drove away from the ranger station. I realized my dream job just became hell. I'd have to work beside my mate on a daily basis.

"Grayson?"

"Huh?" I responded as I turned and looked at Jai.

"There you are. I called your name several times. I asked if everything was okay? You don't seem happy."

"Everything's fine. I was just thinking. So what's so interesting about the south beach of Flathead Lake?"

"It's one of our major touristy areas. There's a large section that is great for swimming, and it attracts a lot of visitors. We have to check it frequently during tourist season to make sure the swim buoys are still in place as well as the nets."

"That makes sense. So we're going to check on those?"

"We can. Honestly, I just thought we should get out of there and away from those two. We wouldn't be able to talk otherwise. As it is, they're going to constantly be picking on us."

"Why would they do that?"

"Because just a few months ago I was complaining about not finding my mate yet and here you are. To think that I could have found you almost a year ago." Jai had a sad look on his face, and it made me want to pull him into my arms and comfort him. What was up with that? Was that part of being mates? My bear was grumbling at me, wanting me to do that exact thing, but I told him to be quiet. Our mate was driving us, and I couldn't hold him just now.

"Yeah, I guess. I'm sorry."

"No need to be sorry. The fates know what they're doing and when it's best that we meet. I'm sure there's a reason we haven't met before now."

"I think you're the only one I haven't met yet. You're a panda, right? I don't quite recognize your scent, but I remember hearing that there was a panda in the den."

"I am, yes. And you're a polar bear. I recognize your scent because I've worked with Troy for the past two years. That and I know all about how you and the rest of your group came to the den." Jai glanced at me and gave me a quick smile before looking back out the windshield. Instead of looking out the passenger window again, I looked out the windshield and watched the scenery from a different perspective, still lost in thought about everything that had happened already this morning.

"Do you have siblings?"

"I do. I have three brothers and five sisters."

"Wow. That's a lot of cubs!" I was surprised. Nine cubs? That was almost unheard of. Did pandas have an easier time getting pregnant?

"Yeah, my omega dad seems to be quite fertile. I'm smack in the middle. Four older, four younger."

"So you have two dads?"

"Yep. Female pandas are just like any other female bear. They have a difficult time getting pregnant. My dads have been mated for almost three-hundred years. Only three of us are left waiting for our mates. Well, now two of us. I have a brother and sister left unmated. Well, and me, until you claim me that is," Jai said as he pulled into a busy parking area. He wasn't kidding when he said it was a popular area.

"When does tourist season end?"

"This is the last weekend so we're going to be extra busy. Labor Day weekend seems to signify the end of summer and most people are trying to get in that last fun-in-the-sun moment before the long, cold winter sets in."

"Makes sense. Should we go have a look around?" I asked as I opened my door. I didn't give Jai a chance to reply before I walked to the front of the truck and waited. I may have been young, but I had manners and knew how to use them. It crushed me that I was going to have to tell Jai I couldn't claim him. I wasn't settled enough for a mate. I had nothing to offer yet.

When the beautiful man joined me in front of the truck and smiled up at me, I did my best to keep an indifferent look on my face. Damn, this was going to be hard.

Jai — 2

Holy shit! My mate was so adorable. And young. So very young. But I could work with that. I had no issues with being mated to someone younger than me. In fact, it could have its advantages. I'd heard stories about young alphas and how they could…no. I was *not* going to let my mind go there. I'd been fighting a hard-on since I heard him growl back at the station. And the wetness I'd felt seeping from my hole didn't help. I was going to have to go home and change once we were finished here.

When I smiled up at Grayson, I tried to not be hurt by his indifferent response. Gone was the adorable smile. What did I do wrong? Was he displeased with me? Did he not want a panda as a mate? Maybe I was too old, and he wanted someone his age.

"I assume the buoys floating out across the water are what we're here to check?" Grayson asked as he pointed to the line of red and white floating buoys.

"Yes. There's a net attached to the bottom of them. It helps keep some of the larger fish out of the swimming area. The smaller ones can pass through, but the larger ones obviously can't. We just have to check the tie-off points on either side and make sure it's still secure. If you follow me, I'll show you what we're looking for."

"Sounds good. Lead the way, Ranger Jai." Grayson held out his right arm in gesture for me to pass. This wasn't exactly going as I'd planned. We needed to get the line checked and then get away from the throng of people so we could have the privacy we needed.

As we approached the first side at the water's edge, I showed Grayson the tie-off and how we checked it.

"Seems simple enough. How often do we check it?"

"At this beach, daily. It doesn't normally come loose, but we have to be sure it stays put. Things happen and if someone were to swim out much further, there's a nasty rip current about twenty yards beyond."

"If the rip current is so close, why is this beach so popular with the tourists?" Grayson asked as he stood up. We'd checked the lines, and they were secure to the tie-off point.

"I think it mostly has to do with the larger beach area. The shore here isn't rocky like other places, and the bottom of the lake isn't mucky. It's full of small pebbles and sand just like the beach," I replied as I picked up a handful of the sand and pebbles. I held my hand out and let the rocks and sand fall from my fist. Grayson stuck his palm below mine and caught some of the falling sand. He let the sand drop from his hand before he looked at me and then quickly away.

"Should we check the other side? I'd really like to get back to the station and find out what my duties are going to be." Not even waiting for me to respond, Grayson gave me a subtle nod before he started around the beach. His boots crunching on the small pebbles made me look down at them, but I quickly looked up, and when I got to his ass, I had to stifle a groan. Now was not the time to get a hard-on. I'd just barely gotten the first one under control. It was only a little after eight in the morning, but already, the beach area was filling up.

I quickly caught up with Grayson, and after we checked the second tie-off, we answered a few questions from visitors before we were on our way back to my truck. Grayson was walking just behind me, and once we reached the side of my truck, he growled quietly, but also forcefully enough to send shivers down my spine. I yelped when he yanked me and forced me behind him.

"Well, well. What do we have here? Do you really think you're a match for me? You're just a cub. But it's cute that you're trying to protect the little omega there."

"Jai, call War. Now," Grayson growled and if I was Arik, I knew I'd purr. As it was, I wanted to bleat and present myself to him so he could claim me here and now. Grayson's arm was still pulling me tightly into his back, so I nodded and pulled out my cellphone to make the call. War picked up almost immediately.

"Hey, Jai. I heard congratulations—"

"Sheriff, you're needed at the south beach immediately. Grayson and some unknown alpha are squaring off, and I don't know how long before they shift and go at each other. The beach is already full of tourists."

"Give me ten. Keep him there and try to keep them calm and from shifting if you can."

War was gone before I could reply, and I didn't want to move because I didn't know if doing so would cause Grayson to become agitated. Right now, he seemed content with me behind him. I didn't want to upset my mate so I stayed put.

"So you think I'm going to just hang out and wait for your sheriff to get here, huh?"

"You have two options. You can stand there and wait for the sheriff to get here, or we can shift and go at it. Your choice."

"That's a serious ultimatum coming from someone so young. You really think you can take me?"

"I know I'm willing to try. I might be young, but that doesn't mean I'm weak."

"You're not going to shift. Not in front of all these humans. What you're going to do though is pass over the omega and let me go."

"Think again. After what your group did to—" The sound of sirens approaching cut Grayson off and gave the other alpha enough of a distraction to be able to turn and run.

"Dammit," Grayson said as he took off after the other alpha. I watched them disappear into the woods, and I desperately wanted to follow and help, but I knew I needed to let War know what happened and where they'd gone. Only, it wasn't War that pulled up. No, it was his deputy, Gage. War wasn't but a few moments behind though. However, he pulled up with his lights on and no siren.

"Dammit, Gage. I said *NO* siren! Where'd they go?" War asked as he looked at me. I couldn't speak so I just grunted and pointed the direction they went. War and Gage took off running, and they too, quickly disappeared in the trees. We'd started to attract the attention of the visitors on the beach, and when several of them went to follow, I knew I had to intervene. Who knew what they'd find.

"Absolutely not! You can either go back to the beach where you were, or you can get in your vehicle and leave the park. You will not interfere with the sheriff and his business."

When an incredibly loud growl was answered with an equally loud one, I decided I needed to close the beach immediately. Shit, this could be bad. The screams and concerned looks from the visitors only intensified when several shots rang out. Yep, time to get everyone out of here, now.

"Alright, everyone. I need you all to quickly gather your things and vacate the area, immediately."

The sound of squealing tires caught my attention, and Troy and Ryker rushed out of the truck and looked at me. When I pointed, they too, took off running towards the tree line. The visitors were rushing to their vehicles, and after hastily throwing their belongings in, and loading up children, they all left in a hurry. Hopefully, they wouldn't attempt to come back. We'd have to close the roads so others couldn't get here, but for now, I needed to know that Grayson was okay.

He hadn't had a chance to claim me yet. Hell, we'd barely had a chance to talk, so I didn't have any way to communicate with him to know if he was okay. So I just stood there, waiting for my den members to return. The last person I expected to see was Arin. Seeing Ryker's mate suddenly appear beside me was unsettling as well as discouraging.

"Hey, Jai. Ryker asked me to take you back to War's place. I'll try my best to land us safely, but just so you know, I still struggle with reentry sometimes."

"What? No. I don't want to leave yet. Grayson is still out there in the woods. Should we go after them?"

"No, Jai. We shouldn't. Grayson and the others will be back soon, if they're not already at the alpha house. War is going to call an emergency den meeting and has asked that all den members be present."

"I can drive my truck—"

I wasn't given any choice, and before I knew it, I was lying on the floor in War's house beside Arin. I knew Ryker's young mate was still learning, but I didn't know how he put up with it. Or how his backside survived.

"Sorry about that. They asked that I get you back here as soon as possible. We didn't have time to stand there and discuss options."

"What's going on?" I asked, just as Arik came running through the room with a bag slung over his shoulder.

"Arin, watch the twins!" And then he was out the door. My head whipped towards Arin who looked like he'd gotten bad news, but when he looked at me, he smiled and got up off of the floor. "Should we go play with Bradley and Harrison? Edwin is napping, but the twins are awake. Linus is with Troy and Elliot's triplets at their place, so we don't have to watch them."

"What? Where's Edwin?"

"He's here. Arik was watching him for me. He's really the calmest baby ever, somehow. Ryker and I got so lucky with him."

I got up off of the floor and followed Arin up the stairs to the nursery. War and Arik's twins ran around the room, playing what looked to be a game of tag. They giggled when they caught up with the other, and then took off in the opposite direction. I couldn't help but smile at them. Would I have cubs some day? Did Grayson even want cubs? Did he want me?

"Don't worry. They're all okay."

"Yeah? That's good to know. Do you know what happened yet?"

"Only bits and pieces. Ryker said War planned on letting everyone know what happened once they all arrived."

"And Grayson? He's okay?"

"Yeah, Jai. He's okay."

Hearing that from Arin was a huge relief. Even if he wasn't yet mine, I needed to see my mate. My panda wanted to curl up with him and cuddle. But we'd take just seeing him and knowing he was okay.

After what felt like hours, but was actually only half an hour at most, the rest of the den members started to arrive. War included. Arin and I each carried a squirmy toddler downstairs and when they saw their dad, they both reached for him at the same time. Alpha War smiled and reached for his boys. With one in each arm, he gave them both a kiss and then walked off towards his office. Troy was directly behind him with Elliot tucked under his arm.

I looked for Grayson, and when I didn't see him, I started to get worried until Ryker approached me.

"He needed to go home and change first, Jai. He's just fine though. You've got yourself a tenacious mate there. He's young, but let's just say that I'm glad he's on our side and not theirs."

"What? Why? You're sure he's alright? Where does he live? What's going on, Ryker? I'm really getting pissed off."

"No need. Actually, I'm told Grayson lives in the small cabin out back here. You go out the back door there, and it's the cabin that's in the back right hand corner of the property. It's right next to the forest out back."

I nodded and took off towards the back door as fast as I could. I needed to see that my mate was okay with my own eyes. My panda wouldn't rest until then.

Grayson — 3

I hurt just about everywhere. Going after the much larger and older alpha probably wasn't my smartest move. Luckily, I'd distracted and held him off long enough that Gage and Alpha War showed up. They both held back and let me go at him, I got in several good swipes, too, but when he got the better of me and had me pinned below him, Gage pulled his pistol and fired off a few shots. The alpha I'd been fighting with was hit, but he quickly ran off, deeper into the woods. Hopefully, he wouldn't stay shifted long as polar bears weren't native to Montana.

When I shifted back to my human self, I had several deep gashes on my back and torso that weren't going to heal quickly without some help.

"Hang on, Grayson. I'll have you back at the house in just a moment and then either Edison or Arik can help."

"Thanks, Alpha." That was the last I remembered and then I woke up with both Alpha Mate Arik and Edison standing over me in my small cabin.

"What happened?"

"You passed out from blood loss. With a little help, you're healed now, so you'll be fine. You should probably take it easy for a few days, but I imagine you won't," Edison said to me. When I looked down, I realized I was in my bed and I was still naked.

"It's up to you, if you want to come to the pack meeting in a few minutes. War's at the house so if you want to join us, we'll see you there. If not, I'm sure your new mate will be more than willing to stay and fuss over you," Arik said as he grabbed a roll of medical tape and stuffed it in his bag before he got up and promptly left. It was a little uncomfortable lying there with Edison standing over me.

"Grayson, can I offer a piece of unwanted advice?"

"Yes, sir," I said as I gingerly sat up. My back was sore, my stomach was sore, and what did I do to my shoulder?

"Don't let age be a factor when it comes to your mate. You only get one, and the fates know what they're doing. You two have been in close proximity to each other for almost a year now. But yet, you haven't met until today. Why do you think that is?"

"I don't know. Bad luck I guess?"

"No, you haven't met until now, simply because you weren't ready. The fates knew that."

"What? And now all of a sudden I am? I have nothing to offer him. I don't even have—"

"Stop. Remember, everything happens for a reason. And if you believe in that, you two will have a lifetime of happiness. But don't let certain things, such as ill-placed honor or preconceived ideas as to what the roles between an alpha and omega should be, come between you. It'll only cause both of you a great deal of pain and suffering," Edison said and then he was gone. Poof, like he was never there.

Immediately following, someone started banging on my door. Thinking it was my Da, and I was going to get my ass handed to me for getting into a fight on my first day of work, I oh so carefully got up off of the couch and padded to the door, naked. I didn't expect to find my mate on the other side though.

"What are you doing here?" I asked, probably a little too harshly since I saw the hurt on his face before he could mask it.

"I wanted to see that you were okay. Everyone said you were, but I still wanted to see with my own eyes."

"I'm fine, as you can see. Unless you're going to the meeting, you should go home, Jai. There's nothing for you to do here. I need to get dressed for the meeting, so if you'll excuse me."

"Grayson? What did I do wrong?"

"Nothing. Why?"

"Then why are you so mad? Am I a disappointment?"

At the devastated look on my mate's face, I just about broke. But I knew that until I had something, anything, to offer him, I wasn't good mate material. I'd heard about all of the struggles my dad and da had gone through when they first mated. Dad was younger than me and had nothing. My parents lived with Dad's parents and siblings. My grandparent's home quickly became crowded with the addition of Da and soon after, my oldest sister.

I wanted more than that. I wanted better for my gorgeous mate. He deserved so much more than a tiny, one-room cabin that wasn't even mine. What little money I had saved over the past couple years I'd spent to buy my used truck. Jai's was fairly new and nice. Mine creaked when you opened the doors. What could I possibly offer him?

Remembering he'd asked a question, I looked down at him and took a deep breath. He smelled so good. The spicy undertones to his scent drove me and my bear crazy. Now was not the time to get a hard-on since I was naked and there was no way of hiding it.

"No, Jai, you're not a disappointment. I just want…I don't think now is a good time is all."

"What do you mean?"

"There's a lot going on with the den right now. You've been here for years and I only joined the den a year ago. I'm twenty-one, Jai. Can you honestly say that my age doesn't bother you? At all?"

"You're young. Nothing wrong with that. For whatever reason, the fates said we were each other's perfect match. Is it me? Am I too old? I know I'd be a good mate. I've wanted—"

"No. That's not it. I'm not ready to mate yet, Jai. I haven't even finished my first day at my first job. Hell, I hope I still have a job after what happened today. I need to get dressed."

Jai let his eyes slowly rove over my body, starting at my face, briefly stopping at my cock—which was taking interest in my mate being so close—and working their way down to my feet. There was nothing I could do about that except put some much-needed distance between us. I took a step back, and when Jai's eyes met mine again, I gave him a curt nod before closing the door and stepping away.

My bear was upset and let me know by demanding I open the door and pull our mate inside with me. Mates were for claiming, cuddling, and taking care of by feeding and protecting according to him. I had to agree. I could do the first two, but I didn't yet have enough of an income to support my mate, and after what happened earlier today, I was unsure if I could protect him. After all, I was the one who walked away with several wounds that required help with healing. Yeah, as a shifter, I had rapid healing capabilities. But they only helped so much. And if we lost too much blood, it wouldn't matter anyway.

After slowly dressing in a clean, non-shredded set of clothes, I walked back to the door and opened it. I tried to not be hurt when Jai was gone, but I didn't blame him. I was an ass and had closed the door on him. What did I expect? I wouldn't have waited around. I needed to talk to Da quick before I completely screwed everything up with my mate.

Making the short walk from my cabin to my Alpha's house was a painful reminder that I should probably be resting and recovering instead of walking to a den meeting. I could have been cuddled up with my mate, but I'd been an ass and sent him away. What was wrong with me?

When I entered Alpha War's house through the back door, all eyes turned to me and I wasn't quite sure why.

"Grayson. Good. Come in and join us. We're waiting for just a few more den members, but come in and have a seat," War said as he gestured for me to enter. I slowly, and somewhat stiffly, walked over to where my parents were and sat down. Almost immediately, Da started fussing at me.

"Grayson, what's wrong? You're acting like you're in pain."

"Just a little twinge here and there. It's nothing."

"You sure? How did your first day at work go?"

"Well, since it's not yet noon and we're all here instead of at work, I'd say, all-in-all, pretty crappy." I met Jai's eyes across the room and saw the hurt look on his face. I'd done that, and I could fix it, but was I man enough to do so?

"Grayson?"

"Huh?" I asked when I heard my dad saying my name. When I looked at him he gave me a somewhat confused look, but Da's look was much more understanding.

"Da? Can we talk later? I have some questions for you."

"You know I'm always here for you children. No matter how old you are, or what the circumstances are."

"Thanks, Da." I gave my carrier a quick kiss on the cheek and got up to cross the room.

"Grayson," Dad said, too harshly since it got the attention of everyone else in the room. I turned and looked at my sire and tried not to get into another argument with him. Any time we'd been near each other over the past few weeks, it seemed all we'd done was argue.

"Yes?"

"Where are you going?"

Shit. It was now or never, wasn't it? But I couldn't do it, could I?

"I'm going to sit with my coworkers. A lot has happened today already, and I'd like to talk with them."

I didn't wait for a response, nor did I offer any more of an answer. I simply turned and left. When I crossed the room, I walked right up to Jai and Ryker, who were sitting on one of the couches with Arin and little Edwin. He sure was adorable.

"Hey, Grayson. Here, let me help and you can sit with us," Ryker said as he reached over and simply plucked Arin up off of the seat and pulled both his mate and baby onto his lap. Edwin never stirred and just continued to sleep in his carrier's arms.

I sat down in between Ryker and Jai. If I was sitting next to anyone other than my mate, I'd say I was sitting closer than necessary, but Jai was mine, and I knew I needed to make sure he realized I wasn't refusing him.

I laid my arm across the back of the couch, and when Jai stiffened beside me, I knew I'd already caused a lot more damage than I realized. With my left hand, I reached for Jai's face and gently turned it towards me.

"I'm sorry. Forgive me, please. Can we talk later?" I asked, and Jai's eyes immediately softened towards me.

"Alright, everyone is here now. First thing, let's all offer our congratulations to Jai and Grayson for finding each other. Hopefully, they'll choose to stay on in Honey Creek and raise their cubs here. If not, I'd like to wish them well. But congratulations you two," War said, and the room immediately was filled with quiet gasps that were followed by squeals and laughter. I leaned in and placed a gentle kiss on Jai's cheek, right next to his ear.

I felt a shiver go through his body before I whispered to him, "Please, Jai, I'm sorry. I promise to try if you'll just give me a chance."

When Jai melted into my side and laid his head on my shoulder, I hoped I was getting my chance. I wrapped my arm around him and pulled him tighter into my side. I ignored the twinge of pain I felt from my healing wounds. I had my mate in my arms, and my bear was finally happy and content. At least, for now.

The few den members who didn't already know about us finding each other came rushing over to congratulate us. When my parents approached, I got up with just a little bit of struggling. I'd hoped nobody noticed, but when I turned to help Jai up, I saw the concerned look on his face.

"Grayson?" Da asked quietly from behind me.

I turned and held tightly to Jai's hand so I could introduce him to my parents.

"Da, Dad, I'd like you to meet my mate. Jai and I scented each other this morning when I arrived at work."

"Grayson, I'm so happy for you. Congratulations you two," Da said to us. He gave Jai a tight hug while Dad gave me a hesitant smile.

"Yeah, Dad, I know."

"What? I didn't say anything."

"You didn't have to," I replied before turning back to my carrier and mate. I wrapped my arm around Jai's shoulders again and pulled him into my side once more.

"You two should come to dinner soon. I don't expect you'll want to come tonight but—"

"No, tonight's great. You two can get to know Jai better. Besides, you and I can talk then?"

Da looked back and forth between me and my mate before he nodded in understanding.

"Of course, tonight sounds wonderful. Does six work for you two?"

"Yeah, Da, six is great." I smiled at Jai who had a confused look on his face. Hopefully, he'd understand and listen to why I wanted to have dinner with my parents before I claimed him.

"Alright, now that the congratulations have been given, let's get on with our meeting," War said. We all settled back into our seats and waited to hear what our Alpha had to say.

Jai — 4

The last thing I expected was to be going to my mate's parents' place for dinner. I'd really hoped I'd be able to talk Grayson into going to my place. When I moved to Honey Creek all those years ago, I knew I'd finally found home. There was just something about the small town that spoke to me. When I didn't find my mate, yeah, I was a little disappointed, but I knew that I was meant to be here. Now I knew why.

The house I'd bought was made for a family, a rather large one, actually. I'd hoped to find a mate and fill it. But when I didn't, I couldn't let the house go because I'd already fallen in love with it. So I'd puttered around a too-big house for several years, hoping that one day my mate would find me. And now he had, except I was unsure if he even wants me.

I sat beside Grayson and snuggled into his side. I could tell he was sore, maybe even hurt, from his earlier altercation with the other alpha. It was Alpha War's comments that brought me out of my thoughts.

"Troy was able to inform us that the alpha that Grayson was engaged with this morning is not Alpha Hank, but one of his sons, Harvey. Grayson, if you'd please let everyone know what happened, I'd appreciate it," War said to my mate who immediately stiffened beside me. I gave his stomach a gentle, yet encouraging, pat, and he smiled at me before getting up. I didn't expect him to pull me up with him though. We walked over to the side of the room where we stopped to stand next to War and Troy. Grayson turned to address the rest of the room.

"There isn't a whole lot to tell really. Jai and I were at the south beach checking the swim buoys. When we were finished, we made our way back to his truck where we were confronted by the unknown alpha. He made some threats and tried to take Jai with him. When Deputy Gage showed up, the alpha took off running for the forest and I followed. Once we'd made it about a hundred or so yards in, he stopped and turned and growled at me. I responded with a growl and when he shifted, I did the same. We'd both gotten some damaging hits in on each other, and when Deputy Gage fired his weapon at the other alpha, he turned and ran. I started to chase him, but Alpha War stopped me. That's the entirety of the situation as far as I know," Grayson said before he looked over at War like *what now*'. I did my best to not chuckle at my mate's questioning face. I somehow managed, but just barely.

"Did Harvey say anything to you while in the woods?" War asked.

"No, Alpha. He growled then shifted. The only conversation I had with him was in the parking lot when Jai was there."

"Very good. Edison, do you have anything you can add to this? I know Grayson's wounds required medical attention, even with his shifter healing. Do you know if Harvey's will as well?"

"Harvey won't make it back to where his den is camped without some sort of help or medical attention, too. Young Grayson here may be younger, but from what I was able to read after the altercation, he held his own and was able to get in some equally damaging swipes. Your deputy's bullets also added to the damage Harvey suffered."

I stiffened beside Grayson, and he simply leaned over and kissed me on the temple and then stood back up. It was almost as if it was second nature for him to do so. But knowing he'd suffered severe wounds that required medical attention, upset me. Shifters almost never required the services of a doctor.

"Was Harvey alone? Or are more of his group with him?" Ryker asked.

"The rest of the group is still up by the Canadian border. I would imagine Harvey was down here doing some snooping for his father," Edison told the room. We all nodded in agreement.

"I feel bad even asking, but will you let us know if they leave their camp and come this way?" War asked his father-in-law.

"I can tell you now that they'll leave their camp within the next couple weeks. When Harvey doesn't return, they *will* come looking for him. When they don't discover him or his body, they'll come here looking for answers."

"Are you saying we need to help Harvey so he can make it back to his group? Because honestly, I'm not feeling any sort of kindness towards him right now," I said as I wrapped my arms around Grayson's waist and held on as if I'd never see him again. My mate leaned down to where my face was nestled into his neck and he could whisper into my ear.

"Shh, I'm okay. I am an alpha, you know," he said before he gave me another quick kiss. This time right on my ear lobe. When I shivered from the contact, he quietly chuckled before pulling away. I was going to die of frustration before my mate actually got around to kissing me for real. I snuggled in and enjoyed Grayson's scent and warmth. I really wouldn't mind if he ended up being a cuddler.

"It won't matter, Jai. If we were to bring Harvey here and help him, the outcome would still be the same. Only with him here, there's more of a chance of someone getting hurt. As it is, from what I've been able to read from his aura, this is his fate," Edison told me. I gave him a slight nod and snuggled back into my alpha's neck. If he was in a comforting and cuddling mood, I'd take it.

It wasn't uncommon for mates to be openly affectionate towards each other. But I realized that Grayson's dads weren't overly affectionate. In fact, they were the only mated pair in the room that weren't even touching. What was up with that? Would Grayson be upset if I asked?

"Edison, do you know how long we'll have before Hank and his group come to attack?" Troy asked.

"I'm sorry, son, no. As of now, all I can say is a couple weeks. If and when I get another feel for it, I'll be sure to let everyone know. The protection spells are also still in place. War, you might want to contact Forest over in Timber Valley and let him know so he and his pack can be on alert. How is Orin doing over there?"

"Last I heard, Orin was doing well. He's having a lot of fun playing with the few pups they have in the pack. But I will give Forest a call as soon as we're finished. If anyone has any questions or concerns, please speak up. As always, I'm available to any of you if you have any questions later," War said to the room. I tuned out the rest of what was being said and just enjoyed the sound of Grayson's heartbeat.

"Hey, don't fall asleep on me while standing up."

"Huh?"

"I think you were starting to doze off. You okay?" Grayson asked, concern in his dark brown eyes.

"Yeah. It's just been an eventful day. That and you smell really good and all that," I said as I pulled away. I looked around the room and several den members were leaving while others were still standing or sitting around talking.

"Would you like to go talk to my parents again? Or maybe go back with Ryker and Arin to the station?"

"I'd like to go with Ryker. I wanted to talk to him about a couple things."

"Okay. I need to ask my da something and then I'll be right over."

"Alright." I smiled at my mate and then walked over to Ryker and Arin. Little Edwin was now in his dad's arms, and Ryker looked completely at home holding the little guy.

"Hey, Jai. Would you like to hold him? He's usually pretty laid back," Ryker offered.

"Thanks, but I'll hold off. I just…I don't…"

"Don't worry, Jai. I get it," Arin said. He looked knowingly towards Grayson and then back at me and smiled. "I'd say you have your work cut out for you. Will he be moving in with you? After all, you have that nice, big house."

"I don't know. We haven't had an opportunity to talk much. Earlier this morning he wasn't very approachable, and then this all happened."

"I don't know, Jai. He seemed pretty stuck on you at the station. Speaking of station, I assume you two will be taking some time off?" Ryker asked.

"I don't know. We're having dinner with his dads tonight, and that's about all I know that's going on. Earlier I didn't even think he wanted me. He said he wasn't ready for a mate, so I don't think you'll have to worry about losing us, or us needing time off."

"How's that going to work? I mean, he's your mate. Isn't being near him going to send you into heat?" Arin asked.

"I'm not sure. I just had it a couple months ago. That's why I went to California. That's *not* a conversation I'm looking forward to having with him."

Arin cringed at my statement, and I internally groaned as I smelled my mate near me.

"We can talk about that later, Jai. Ryker, would it be okay if we took the rest of the day off? Edison said I should take it easy for a few days, and there's some things I want to discuss with *my mate*. We'll both be in tomorrow morning on time," Grayson said. Holy shit! Jealous Grayson was even hotter!

"Are you sure you two won't need a week? Most couples need about a week when they claim each other," Ryker asked while looking between the two of us.

"Yeah, when we get to that, I'll let you know. As of now, I want to get to know Jai a little better and make sure I'm what he really wants before I claim him. I want him to have a say in it. Especially since I know I'm so much younger than him."

"That's quite honorable, Grayson. But realize that Arin and Arik are both quite a bit younger than me and War. In fact, they're only eight years older than you. The fates know what they're doing, and they wouldn't have paired the two of you if you weren't perfect for each other," Ryker told my mate. He nodded before sighing.

"I know. I just feel as if he got the short end of the deal. I mean, I have nothing," Grayson said while looking at me. His cheeks were tinged pink, and I had a better understanding of the conflict he was experiencing.

"Don't worry, mate. Things will work out. Can we maybe go somewhere and talk? I think we have a lot to discuss."

"That'd be good. Da is looking forward to having us for dinner tonight. You can meet my sister. She's in school right now, so she's not at the meeting."

"That'd be great. I can't wait to get to know more about you and your family."

"You two take a few days and then let me know what's what. If you need more time, Troy and I will cover it. Don't worry about it. And Grayson, your job is secure so don't worry about that. Alright?"

"Thanks, Ryker. I appreciate it."

"You ready?" Grayson asked as he looked at me and smiled.

"I am. Lead the way and I'll follow."

"Nope, you'll walk right beside me. Come on, I want to tell to you a few things before dinner." Grayson grabbed my hand and pulled me away from the rest of the group and towards the door. Maybe I was finally going to get invited into his cabin?

Grayson — 5

What was I thinking? Actually, I know what I was thinking. I was letting my bear make decisions, and he was pushing me to claim our mate. I couldn't blame him. Jai was so beautiful and sweet. Add in what Edison said about not letting our ages keep me from him, I was a goner. I needed to talk to Da and get some advice before anything could happen, but I also needed to not hurt my mate any more than I already had.

I grabbed Jai's hand and interlaced our fingers together as we walked from the Alpha's house to my cabin. I didn't have much of anything at there, but at least it wasn't my parent's house.

"Whatcha thinking about over there?"

"Not much. Just that I don't have much at the cabin yet. I just moved in this past weekend and most of my things are still in boxes."

"Oh. Is that why you didn't want me to come in earlier?"

"No. Earlier I was just being an ass and I'm sorry. There was also the fact that you're my mate, and I can't help but find you attractive." Jai blushed at my comment, and I felt better for saying it. I needed to remember to always compliment him. I knew he was older, but I wasn't quite sure how much older, not that it truly mattered when it was all said and done. For whatever reason, the fates had decided he was perfect for me, and I wasn't going to complain or second guess them.

"Well, I find you attractive, too. I like it that you're taller than me."

I turned to Jai just as we reached my cabin's door and noticed his cheeks were bright red under his tan complexion and it was adorable. Placing a finger under his chin, I gently turned his face up and towards me. "Trust me, I'm happy to be taller than you. Or that you're shorter than me. Either way, it's the same and works for me." I smiled before I let go of his chin and then opened the door. "Here you go. It's not much, but at least it's not my parents' house."

"What's wrong with your parents' house?" Jai asked as he entered the cabin. I walked several feet into the one-room space and then stopped.

"Nothing, really. Except that it's my parents' place. At least here I have privacy. I do have drinks if you'd like one. Perhaps we could sit and spend some time together?" I asked while gesturing towards the couch I'd woken up on earlier. It was probably a good thing I wasn't in the bed up in the loft. At the time, the thought of going up and down the ladder made me cringe. I was already feeling better, but I still wasn't back to a hundred percent yet.

"Water would be fine if you have glasses. Otherwise, I'm good."

"I do. Do you want ice?"

"No. Just water is fine. Grayson, you don't have to be nervous. I'm not going to jump on you or anything if that's what you're worried about."

"I know. In some ways, maybe that would be easier," I mumbled as I walked towards the kitchen area. When I turned with two cups in my hands, I dropped them when I almost collided with Jai who had walked up behind me without me knowing.

"Don't forget, just because I'm a panda doesn't mean I don't have shifter hearing as well," he said right before he wrapped his arms around my neck and jumped up onto me. Instinctively, my hands found his small, yet firm ass, and I couldn't hold the groan that escaped me. Because I had my mate wrapped around me and I felt a twinge in my still-healing shoulder. "I don't know any more about mating than you do. Not really. I know my parents have been together for several centuries and that they are still very much in love with each other. It's almost as if they claimed each other just yesterday."

"I wish I had parents like that. Mine are fated, obviously. But some days, I wonder if my dad even likes my da. He's often distant and I just don't understand him."

"Hmm, that doesn't mean you'll be the same. You've already been very affectionate towards me," Jai said as he ran his nose along my neck and jaw. I walked to the couch and sat with him still wrapped around me. He quickly moved his legs so he was straddling my lap, and when I looked into his brown eyes that were shimmering with happiness, I knew I needed a taste of his soft-looking lips.

"Jai, please."

"Please, what?"

"Can I kiss you?"

"You don't have to ask. I've been dying to know what your kiss feels like."

I gently cupped Jai's face and pulled his mouth to mine. When our lips first met, I felt a zing go through my body and straight to my dick. At times, it really was unfair that I was so young, and it didn't usually take much to get me excited. With my fated mate placed in my lap, it was a guarantee. I still had a hold of Jai's ass so I pulled him tighter to me, and when our denim-covered cocks collided, we both moaned loudly. I swiped my tongue across his lips, and when he readily opened, I gently probed his mouth. Our tongues gently mated, and when I got a whiff of his spicy arousal, I reluctantly broke the kiss and pulled back.

"Can we do that again?" Jai asked and leaned in for another kiss. I obliged but kept it short and sweet. When I pulled away again, I cleared my throat before looking at Jai.

"It's not that I don't want you. I know you can feel how much I do. I just want to wait a little longer. I want to know more about you, and you me, before we go any further."

"Alright. But I want to know something. Do you plan on claiming me?"

"Yes, Jai. I do. But not right now. Not here where I don't even have food to feed you afterward, let alone my stuff unpacked. I have one towel in the bathroom, and that's only because I didn't pack it. I just threw it in the truck and brought it over. I'm simply not ready or prepared for a mate. I never expected to find you so early. And I want so much more for you than my da got from my dad. They lived with dad's parents and siblings when they first mated. I don't want that," I confessed as I buried my face in his neck and gave it a gentle kiss. He moaned while tilting his head to the side to give me better access to the spot where I'd place his claiming bite.

"You know, we could always live in my house. I bought it a long time ago, and it's plenty big enough for the two of us, as well as any cubs we are blessed with."

I stilled at Jai's suggestion, but only because I was so very tempted. But as alpha, wasn't it my responsibility to provide for my mate?

"Jai, it's not that I'm not tempted, because I am. But I just can't. I'm supposed to provide for you. Not the other way around."

"Okay, so that's your dad talking, right? It's my understanding that if we're going with stereotypes, then you provide and protect me while I make the home and whelp the kids. Well, I've made the home, I just haven't gotten the opportunity to have any kids yet," Jai fumed as he climbed off my lap and quickly made his way to the door.

He went through it, but the door slamming was what finally got my ass up and moving to chase my mate. Dammit. That did not go how I wanted it to. When I raced out the door, Jai was nowhere in sight. I ran around the house but collided with Ryker before I could catch up with my wayward mate.

"I see you pissed off Jai already. What'd you do?" Ryker asked as he grabbed my arm to keep me from following. I tried to pull free, but he shook his head and wouldn't release me. "Nope. I don't know Jai nearly as well as Troy does, but I do know he's really upset, and it's probably best to let him cool off for a little while before you go to apologize."

I groaned and looked up to the sky and hoped I'd find my answers. No such luck.

"So, what'd you do?"

"I told him the truth; I don't have anything, Ryker. I haven't even finished my first day of work. How am I supposed to provide for a mate if I haven't even gotten a paycheck yet? I have probably twenty dollars to my name, and that's it until I get paid. I'm twenty-one, what could he possibly see in me?"

"Well, you're his mate so age doesn't really matter. You have to understand, when mates find each other, there's no longer a you and him or her. It's now the two of you in a combined, united pair. I know for a fact that Jai has a house and it's flippin' huge."

"Flippin'? Really?"

"Hey, don't knock it. I'm trying to keep my language clean for Edwin. Arin would put my balls in a vise if Edwin's first word is fuck."

I groaned at the thought. Ryker was right though. If I was going to mate with Jai—no, not if, when—when I mated with Jai, we were going to eventually have cubs of our own. I needed to work on cleaning up my language as well. "Okay, point. But back to Jai's house. How do you know it's huge?"

"Because I've been there. So has Troy. When he moved here, he fell in love with this gorgeous cabin out on the lake. It's huge, Grayson. I think the thing probably has five or six bedrooms. He loves it out there. It's private and secluded, and he can go swimming right off his back deck."

"Really?"

"Yeah. He was drawn to this area. When he didn't find his mate, he said something told him to stay put, so he did. Anything else you should hear from him. But I will say this, there's absolutely no reason why you shouldn't move in with him. That place is perfect for the two of you to raise a family of cubs. Just because it was his place before he met you, that doesn't mean it can't become your family home."

"Fine. Even if I move in with him, I still haven't got anything to offer."

"Sure you do. Yourself. Jai is a lot older than you, but when he was first starting out, he was in the same position. He's just had longer to prepare for things. Don't let it bother you. No matter what, you can always provide him with the most important thing a mate can offer."

"What's that?"

"Yourself. He only needs you, Grayson. I saw you taking on that older alpha. You're pretty badass for such a young alpha. You held your own, and your bear is no joke. I have no doubt that you could protect Jai and any cubs you two will have. But he needs you, your love, your understanding, and your protection. Those are qualities that make a good mate. Yes, you'll get there when it comes to providing for him. But it's okay if he's the provider at first. It doesn't matter who's buying the food. If you both cook, you are both providing for each other. There's so much more to being mates than who provides financially and who doesn't."

"I know that. I just didn't have the greatest example growing up."

"Yes, I've heard about your dads. But I also know that your omega father has views that are very different from those of your alpha father."

"Yes, which is why I'm hoping to talk to him before I claim Jai."

"If you still have any questions after talking to him, know that you can always come to me. I'll answer any questions you have. I'm sure Troy or War would as well."

"Thanks, Ryker. Do you think you could give me Jai's address? I need to get back to the station and pick up my truck, but then I'm pretty sure I need to head out to his place and apologize."

"You're probably right. I was headed back to the station myself, so I'll give you a lift. We'll stop in town and you can get your mate some flowers. It might help."

"Flowers? Really?"

"Couldn't hurt. Arin loves flowers. Although, he's more partial to potted plants. They don't have to be thrown out after a week."

"Maybe I can get him an orchid or something. They're pretty and I like them."

"Let's see what we can find, then. Come on, let's go."

"Don't you have to say bye to Arin?"

"Nope. I already kissed him and Edwin goodbye. I'll see them this evening at home, and I can always talk to him through our mate bond."

"Thanks, Ryker. I really appreciate this."

"Grayson, it's quite alright. It's what den members do. We help when needed."

We walked to Ryker's truck and climbed in and then were on our way. I had some groveling to do, and I hoped it worked and my mate forgave me. *Again.*

Jai — 6

I absolutely couldn't believe my mate. I understood he was young, but that was supposed to work in my favor I thought. Grayson was a younger generation so he was supposed to be more forward thinking. Not have the backwards ideas that an omega was only good for having kids.

I'd always felt that there was so much more to life than just having children. Sure, I wanted kids. I mean, very few shifters didn't. But with Grayson and his views, I was beginning to think I would be lucky if I could get him to claim me.

It felt so amazing to be in his arms. And then his kisses? It was difficult to decide which were more intense; the sweet, quick kisses to my temple and neck, or the long, lingering ones that claimed me. I wanted more of both, but who knew if I'd get either.

Yes, I should have stayed and talked things out instead of storming out like I did, but I didn't want to say something I'd regret. And I needed some time to cool off, or that was going to happen. So I left and did the only thing I could think of. I called my omega dad to ask for some much-needed advice.

"Bà, I met my mate," I said just as soon as he answered the phone.

"Érzi! That's fantastic! Your bàba isn't here right now. He's just gone to work. Do you want us to come visit? What's his name? When did you meet? Are you already pregnant? Oh, érzi, I'm so excited for you!"

I couldn't help it, I laughed at my omega father's excitement for my good fortune. "Slow down, Bà, I said I met my mate. That's all."

"What do you mean, that's all? I need answers, Jai. Stat."

I couldn't help it, I rolled my eyes at him. He was so funny with the slang he was always trying to use. "Okay, let's see if I can remember all the questions. First, his name is Grayson, and he's a polar bear."

"Oh, a polar bear, huh? I bet he's sexy."

"Please, Bà, I'm trying here but you're being…well…you."

"Fine, continue. My lips are zipped."

"Okay, so, he's a polar bear and is so adorable. He's young though, Bà. So young."

"How young?"

"He just turned twenty-one." Bà could be heard whistling through the phone. I once again rolled my eyes at him. He was just too much sometimes. "You finished yet?"

"Jai, you are so blessed! Do you know how fortunate it is that you've got such a young mate? Think of how passionate, how much endurance, and how sensual he'll be. Did I mention endurance? Oh my, yes. You're lucky indeed."

I groaned and regretted calling. "Bà, I'm going to go. I don't want to have this conversation with you."

"What? No! You haven't told me everything yet. I promise, I'll shut up. Really, I will this time."

"Fine. But one more peep and I'm done."

"Deal. Proceed."

"So I told you his name and age. He's the new park ranger at work. We scented each other first thing this morning. We haven't mated yet. We just met. And because he's so young, he seems to have reservations. He's worried about being able to provide for me and any cubs we may have. I mean, I get it, but it's still frustrating. We were talking, but I left when he told me he wanted to wait to claim me. He needs to know he could provide for us financially. He just moved out of his parents' house and into this tiny one-room cabin near the Alpha's house. So he's feeling a little disadvantaged right now. I tried to tell him I already had a house that would be perfect for a family, but he started spouting that provider nonsense. So what do you think, Bà? I'm at a loss. I got upset and left before I said something I regretted."

"Well, that was wise on your part. We both know you can tend to have a bit of a temper."

"So not helping, Bà."

"I was getting there. I'm a little baffled by his thinking. It's almost as if he were the older one in the relationship. Do you know, are his parents older?"

"From what I've heard, his omega dad is older than his alpha dad. But his alpha dad doesn't really seem to know how mating works, and they've been mated for fifty years."

"That's tough. And you mentioned he's a polar bear. I'd say he's probably from one of the old, traditional dens up north somewhere. Did he move to Montana because of the ranger service?"

"No. He arrived with his parents and sister. His dad, Ivan, got them out of there when their dens were attacked."

Bà gasped and I knew he remembered the story when I told him. "That was them? But if his alpha dad did all that, why are there issues?"

"His alpha dad was only twenty when he met his omega dad. They mated right away, and that's about all I know. Grayson said they lived with his alpha father's parents for a while, but then they finally got a place of their own. We didn't really get much of a chance to talk. I called you hoping for some words of wisdom."

"Well, he's your mate. And instinctively, mates, especially the alpha, want to please their omega. Even if they've got an older, more traditional way of thinking, they still want to make their omega happy. When it comes down to it, he will eventually do what he needs to in order to please you. Just be patient. I know it's difficult and if he waits too long, you're going to go into heat now that you've met your fated mate."

I groaned at the thought; I'd just gone through one. That's why I was in California visiting my parents recently. My omega dad helped by making sure we were fed and had all the supplies we needed. It was uncomfortable to go through a heat without an alpha. Bà knew what we were going through and was a great help. Bàba and my alpha brother left and went on a vacation up the coast for a week. Sometimes my unmated sisters went with them, sometimes they stayed home.

"I know you don't like the idea of going through another heat so soon, but I promise, it'll be so much more enjoyable with your alpha there with you. He may be young, but instinct will take over, and he'll take care of you."

"How long do you think I'll have before that'll happen?"

"I would say you'll have a few days at most. And if he claims you before it starts, it'll set it off, and you'll go into heat immediately."

"Okay, so you're saying turn around and hit the grocery store before I make it all the way home?"

"That would be most advisable."

I quickly made a U-turn once I reached the road I lived on. I was a minute away from my place, but Bà was right. I needed a lot more food in the house. The quick kind that a young alpha could just grab and eat and feed me in a hurry. I loved to cook, but I didn't think that Grayson would be thinking about cooking while he was tending to me while I was in heat.

"Okay, Bà, thanks for everything. I'll call you again once I'm mated. I'm headed back to town now to stock up on some supplies. I'll let you know about visiting later. Right now, I'd consider it a small victory if I could get him to agree to mate with me. And we still have some issues brewing with the other Alpha from that pack I was telling you about." The last thing I wanted to do was upset or worry my bà. He was great and so open when it came to talking about everything, but like all parents, he tended to worry.

"He'll come around. Don't worry. Take care, érzi."

"You too, Bà." I ended the call as I drove back to town to visit the local grocery store. I needed to stock up on several things. I was tempted to call and ask Grayson what he liked, but decided against it and figured that, in the moment, he wouldn't care too much. After filling a cart full of items I wouldn't normally have in my pantry, I loaded them in the back seat of my truck and made the drive to my place again.

By the time I had the shelves stocked, it was well past lunch, so I fixed myself something to eat. Unfortunately, that didn't take nearly enough time, and I resorted to basically pouting while lying on my couch and thinking about my mate. I needed to call Ryker and get Grayson's number. We hadn't exchanged numbers, and I didn't know how to get in contact with him. Once we were mated, we would have the mate bond and wouldn't need cell phones to communicate with each other. But until then, I was on my own.

Just as I dug out my phone to call Ryker, my doorbell rang. I almost never had visitors so I was surprised. I got an even bigger surprise when I opened the door and saw Grayson standing on the other side holding a potted orchid. How did he know they were my favorite flower?

"Grayson?"

"Jai, I'm sorry. I was an ass and I'm sorry. It seems I'm just an ass where you're concerned. I keep doing everything wrong. Here. I got you this. I know it doesn't fix what I did, but I wanted to say I was sorry. And show you I was thinking about you."

I took the orchid and stepped back to invite my mate inside. Maybe if he saw the house, he'd be more agreeable to consider living here and raising a family with me in it. "Would you like to come in?"

"You don't mind?"

"Why would I mind? Grayson, you're my mate. You'll always be welcome here."

Grayson finally stepped into the house, and I could tell he liked what he saw. His eyes roved over the decorations and pictures on the walls, and he smiled in appreciation. I had pictures of my family as well as of a few of the places I'd traveled. On the tables, I had figurines that would need to be put up once I had cubs, but I didn't mind. I'd rather have the cubs than a bunch of items I had to dust on a regular basis.

"Would you like a tour? I can show you around if you'd like. Or you're more than welcome to explore on your own. Did you eat? I can fix you something for lunch if you're hungry."

"Jai, it's fine. I ate with Ryker a little while ago."

I was a little disappointed since I wouldn't get to cook for my mate yet. Maybe soon. "Would you like to sit on the back deck? It's beautiful out there, and it's one of my favorite places. I spend a lot of time there and the sunroom. Which is where I'll put this beauty." I turned and walked to my sunroom, and when I got to the door, I realized that Grayson was directly behind me, so I let him enter before me. He abruptly stopped just inside the door but moved when I gave him a little nudge so I could enter and close the door.

"Wow. I guess an orchid was a good choice. Although, you already have so many, so what's one more?"

"Yes, I do. Orchids are my favorite flower. But until now, I haven't been given one by my mate. So your gift is extra special," I replied as I sat the Galeopetalum Starburst Parkside on a shelf in the sunny and warm room. I had dozens of orchids in here. They were what I filled my time with and helped to keep me from being so lonely.

"So, I did okay?"

"Are you kidding? You did great."

"The lady that sold it to me said they're difficult to take care of so to expect that there is a good chance that the person I was giving it to would kill it. I think she's wrong."

"I've only ever lost one or two over the years. One was because it was too far gone when I got it, and I couldn't nurse it back to health. Another was because I knocked it off the shelf and the node broke."

"Well, I'm glad I made a good choice. Can we talk? I want this to work, Jai. And not just because fate deemed us perfect for each other. I want so much more than my parents have."

"Grayson, I promise, we *will* have more. The fact that you're willing to work at it already proves as much. Come on, we'll go sit on the deck and talk." I pulled my mate out of the sunroom and towards my deck so we could talk.

Grayson — 7

My mate was so beautiful. And understanding. I was positive I'd screw up again, but I was thankful he was being patient with me. We spent hours talking on his back deck, and I knew there was no way I could ask him to move. His house was perfect for a family.

Before either of us realized, it was time for dinner with my parents. When Jai went to climb into my truck, I stopped him.

"Would it be okay if we take yours? Mine still has a lot of my stuff in it that I haven't had a chance to unpack yet."

"Oh, sure. Did you want to drive? You know where you're going so that would probably be better."

"I could just give you directions. I'm not one of those alphas that always have to be in control of everything. You've been driving longer than I've been alive. I'm sure you know what you're doing. And besides, you drove us this morning."

"Okay. Well, hop in then and tell me where I'm going."

It seemed that in no time, we were pulling into my parents' driveway. I was anxious to talk to my da about a few things, but at the same time, I was also nervous. My dad just viewed things differently, and I often didn't understand him. Thankfully, Da came out the front door with a huge smile on his face and open arms. He met us at the truck and gave Jai a hug before me.

"I see how it is. Hug the new guy first," I joked with them. Jai gave me a smile while Da gave me a mock glare.

"For your information, I've been giving you hugs for years, young man. Jai here is new. Welcome to the family, Jai. Come in, you two. Dinner is ready, so we can eat whenever you'd like."

"Now would be great, Da. It seems that lunchtime was so long ago." Da rolled his eyes at me, but I saw the smile on his face.

"I hope you're ready to spend a lot of time in the kitchen, Jai. But be sure you make your mate help. All of my children, alpha, omega, female, or male, have all learned to cook. And they clean, for that matter. But this one, he's still young and still eats like a growing cub."

"That's good to know. I happen to love cooking and baking. It'll be nice to have someone to share meals with some of the time."

After Da gave Jai a strange look, Da turned and glared at me. I gave him what I hoped was a "give me a few" look but who knew. We walked into the house and almost immediately, my younger sister, Cassie, came bouncing at us.

"Grayson! I'm so happy you're back. You're staying, right? Please tell me you're moving back in."

"Cassie, I'm just here for dinner."

"What? Why? I want you to move back home. It's not the same without you here. Dad is always grumbling and…" Cassie broke off when she finally noticed Jai standing next to Da. "Who's that?"

"Rude much? Cassie, I want you to meet my mate, Jai. Jai, this is my bratty younger sister, Cassie," I said as I wrapped an arm tightly around Jai's shoulders. There was no way I wanted my mate to think I was even considering moving back home. Cassie, on the other hand, looked like a fish stuck out of water and stood there and opened and closed her mouth. My mate, bless him, approached my sister and gave her one of his charming smiles.

"Hi, Cassie. I'm pleased to meet you. I have five sisters, but none of them live near here. I hope we can get to know each other better."

"Really, Grayson? You found your mate?"

"Yep. And you could at least say hi. You're still being rude, Cassie."

"It's alright, Grayson. I—"

"Well, I mind. There's no reason for her to be rude." Cassie finally realized what she was doing and turned bright red before she looked at Jai and apologized.

"I'm so sorry. I just can't believe he found his mate. I mean, we've lived here for a year already and nothing. I didn't mean to be rude. Please forgive me."

"Don't worry about it, Cassie. Like I said, I have five sisters. I'm not unused to how the female mind works."

I pulled Jai back to me, his back to my front, and wrapped my arms around his chest. Now that I'd accepted the fact Jai was my mate, no matter how much I tried, I wasn't going to be able to deny my bear for too much longer. He was going to win, and I was going to claim our mate.

"Okay, you three. Dinner is ready, as I've already said. Cassie, go tell your dad while I grab everything and place it on the table."

Cassie took off, and before I could offer to help, Jai was pulling out of my arms and following my da to the kitchen.

"If you tell me where I can wash my hands, I'd be happy to help."

"You're welcome to wash your hands in the bathroom there, or at the sink in the kitchen. But you don't need to help. Cassie already set the table; I just have to take the three dishes to the dining room. Grayson, help your mate in the bathroom," Da said so I shrugged my shoulders and pulled Jai into the bathroom. I wrapped him in my arms and gave him a lingering kiss before I broke it and smiled at my stunned little panda.

"Sweetheart, we need to wash our hands. But I'd be more than willing to pick up where we're leaving this a little later," I said as I bent down and gave Jai another little kiss on his neck.

"Yes. Later. Spend the night? Wait, did you just call me sweetheart?"

"Only the night? I thought you said your house was perfect for our family? I figured you'd want me to move in. If you just want a night here and there, I'm definitely going to rethink this whole claiming and oomph..." I wasn't expecting the shove to my abs, or the glare from my fiery mate. I was realizing that he definitely had some sass to him. Life was going to be fun with him by my side.

"Never mind. I've changed my mind. You can go back to your little cabin, and I'll go back to my place."

"Hmm, you sure about that?" I asked as I grabbed his ass and pulled our groins together. Jai was just as hard as I was, and he moaned as I leaned in and gently nibbled on his neck. "We really need to wash our hands. Da went to all the trouble to prepare dinner. We should join them. Besides, my parents' downstairs bathroom is not where I had in mind to claim you."

I pulled away again and went to the sink. After quickly washing my hands, and splashing some cold water on my face, I gave my stunned mate a quick kiss and left the bathroom. He'd be out when he was ready, hopefully.

"I was just about to send Cassie after you two. But from the smell coming from you, I'd say I know what took you two so long," Da said and gave me a knowing smile.

"What? You told me to help Jai in the bathroom. I happened to give him a kiss or two and that's it."

"Do you really expect me to believe that, Grayson? Really?" Da asked.

"What? I promise. I just gave him a couple kisses." I was saved when Jai joined us, and he looked completely calm and collected. How did he do that? I know he was as turned on as I was. He needed to share his tricks.

"Grayson, I put Jai down with you. I hope that's okay," Da said, sounding unsure.

"It's perfect, Da. Where's Dad?" Just as I asked, my alpha father walked into the dining room.

"Grayson, I didn't quite expect you to be back so soon. I thought you were moving out into your own place."

"I am. You know—"

"Ivan, we have one son left alive. Don't be an asshole. I've put up with your disinterest long enough. Grayson and his mate are here for dinner. You know this. You also know that Grayson has a lot of questions regarding being mates, and I won't let him go through this not knowing things just because that was the way you and your backwards den were. We are supposed to help our children. Now sit down, be nice, and shut up, or you can leave."

I really wished we were already mated right about now. I glanced at him and he had a concerned look on his face. I needed to reassure Jai that this was fairly normal for my parents but without our mate bond, I couldn't do so without the others knowing. So I reached over and grabbed his hand and gave it a tight squeeze. Dad decided to listen to Da for once and plopped down in his seat. Dinner was good, but the tension between my parents was certainly noticeable. Da and Cassie were already in love with Jai and were anxious to learn all they could about him, his family, and his bear. After dinner, Cassie dragged Jai off out back while Dad grumbled about something and went to his office. That gave me the perfect opportunity to speak with Da.

"Grayson, I know you wanted to chat, but I don't think you really need to. Jai seems to know what he's doing, and I'm sure you'll make the right choices."

"I've been thinking about it a lot, Da, and I believe you're right. I do have a question though. I thought the fates were supposed to be all-knowing. Why is it that Dad seems so unhappy and disinterested? I don't understand. I've closely watched Alpha War, Troy, and Ryker with their mates and none of them treat their mates like Dad does you. I guess that's my biggest concern. I know Dad expects me to be that way with my mate, but I just can't do it.

I want to hold him and show all kinds of affection. I want to laugh with him and go for long walks in the woods in our bear forms together. I want all of that and so much more. And because of that, Dad sees me as a disappointment."

"Grayson. Listen to me when I tell you that you're not a disappointment. You're a good son and a wonderful alpha. You're exactly like you should be and don't let Ivan sway you otherwise."

"But, Da, I don't want to mess anything up."

"Grayson, if you listen to your heart, you won't. It won't lead you astray. Everything happens for a reason, and Jai was meant to be yours. Yes, you're a lot younger than him. Actually, I think I might be younger than him, but it doesn't matter. What matters is that he'll be a wonderful mate for you. I can tell. And if you have any questions, I'm sure he can probably answer them better than I can. He would know better than I would what exactly he wants from a relationship between you two."

At Da's statement, I had my lightbulb moment and realized he was exactly right. Yeah, I was the alpha in the relationship, but my mate would be the one to enlighten me as to what he needed from me emotionally. I could protect him and our cubs, of that I had no doubts, but I needed to know that I could give him everything else he needed from me.

Already, Jai loved affection. He never shied away from it. In fact, he always gravitated towards me, seeking more. So instead of spending a quiet evening alone with my new mate, I was at my parents' house having an awkward dinner.

"Something clicked, didn't it?"

"Yeah," I replied as I looked up at my Da. I felt so bad for him because I felt he'd been given such a shitty mate. My dad was a good provider and protector, but that's where it ended. He simply wasn't affectionate. And that made me sad for my da. "Da, I'm going to take Jai home. We'll see you next week sometime."

"Next week sounds good. I'm so proud of you, Grayson. Don't ever think otherwise."

"I won't, Da. Next time, everyone needs to come out to Jai's for dinner. You'd love it there."

"You're probably right. But is it Jai's place?"

"Yeah, I guess it's our place, huh? It's just going to take some getting used to."

"All in time. We'll see you two next week." Da gave me a quick kiss and then I went to collect my mate so I could take him home and finish what we'd started on the couch in my cabin and then in the bathroom here.

Jai — 8

Dinner with Grayson's parents was interesting. I wanted to ask so many questions, but I felt it wasn't really my place to do so. I was still a little unsure as to my relationship with Grayson, and I didn't want to make anything worse by asking something that made him uncomfortable.

"Hey, you're quiet over there."

"Sorry. I was just thinking about dinner."

"Yeah, about that. I'm sorry about my dad. He's just difficult most of the time. I don't know how my da has put up with him for so long. I guess it's the whole fated mate thing or something. I know I would be irritated if I had to deal with him like that."

"Don't apologize, Grayson. It happens. For whatever reason, the fates thought your parents were perfect for each other. Maybe it's that Sam is so much more open and outgoing than Ivan, and he sort of balances him out."

"Maybe, I don't know. Da was often so sad when I was growing up. And after Cassie, his heats stopped so he couldn't have any more children so it added to his sadness."

I quickly glanced over at Grayson and then back at the road. I knew where I was going, but it was already dark out, and you never knew when critters would end up in front of your vehicle. Especially out at the lake where I lived.

"Well, maybe there's a reason why. Maybe it was time to play with grandkids. Or maybe his body just got tired. Who knows."

"He used to play with my nieces and nephews, but when we were attacked…"

I reached across the seat and grabbed Grayson's hand and gave it a squeeze. I was sure it had to have been difficult to have lost so much of your family.

"How many siblings do you have?" I realized I hadn't yet asked that question, and now I was curious how many were lost to the ruthlessness of those like Alpha Hank.

"There were five of us, total. Cassie and I are the youngest, and I was actually picking her up from school on my way home from the park when we were attacked. Usually, attacks like that come in the middle of the night, but Hank was confident we wouldn't fight back or live, so he attacked mid-afternoon. Dad fought and held them off long enough for Da to get away to safety. I arrived back right at the height of the attack and grabbed Cassie and ran. We found Da and a couple other families hiding out in the middle of nowhere, basically. It was late spring and was still cold so we all shifted to keep warm. Da was convinced that Dad would find us and he did a day later. We started our trek southward and ended up here. We found Linus and his parents along the way. They were the only couple in their area, and they had an omega son, so they were concerned after they'd heard about the attack on the omegas and their families. Dad offered for them to travel with us, and they joined our group. A few weeks later, we finally made it here to Montana. I guess the rest you know." Grayson looked at me with sorrow-filled eyes.

My poor baby-alpha. He'd been through so much at such a young age. He'd lost three of his siblings and their mates and cubs. All because he came from a family with an omega dad and some traditional spouting asshole deemed them less. We'd been sitting in the driveway for a good ten minutes before Grayson realized we were home.

"When did we get here?"

"A while ago. It's no big deal though. The house will still be there when we go inside."

"Can we?"

"Can we, what?"

"Go inside?"

"Oh, sure. I was just waiting until you were ready," I replied as I opened my door and got out of the truck. Grayson was right behind me, and I could feel the heat from his body as I walked towards the house. "I should probably put the truck in the garage, actually."

"Yeah, that might be good," Grayson said as he stared at his own truck that was parked beside mine.

"Did you still want to stay?" I asked, thinking he wanted to leave.

"Is the offer still open?"

"You're my mate, Grayson. The offer will always be open. Unless you're just wanting a quick fuck, you're welcome here. But if that's what you want, go find it elsewhere because I'm not interested." I tried to storm off again, but this time, Grayson's loud growl stopped me in my tracks. The last time he'd growled that way was this morning. Damn, was that really only just this morning? I slowly turned looking for the threat, but I didn't pick up on anything. When I turned enough to face Grayson, I realized my mistake. I'd pissed off my alpha and damn was he hot as fuck when he was pissed.

"Take. It. Back. Now." Grayson growled out at me. A shiver went through my body, my cock instantly hardened, and my hole flooded with slick. My body felt tingly all over, and I knew that my mate could smell my arousal by the way his nostrils were flaring.

"Grayson, I'm sorry. I know you'd never cheat on me. And you have to know I'm interested. I mean, I'm a mess right now because you're all growly and hot and sexy and all alpha-y." My mate cut me off with a kiss, but this one wasn't nearly as sweet as the one from earlier. No, with this one, Grayson claimed me. Even if he hadn't yet bit me while knotted inside me, he completely claimed my heart and soul with this kiss.

"Mine. My mate."

"Yes, yours. All yours. Always." I tried to reassure my mate, but he slammed his mouth back down on mine and then picked me up. I immediately wrapped my legs around his hips and whimpered when my cock once again collided with his. I wish we weren't wearing any clothing so I could feel his hard body next to mine without the barriers. I found myself flat on my back on the hanging daybed that was on the back deck. Grayson was fascinated by it, and we'd spent a great deal of time lying on it this afternoon talking.

"Grayson, off," I mumbled as I tugged at my mate's shirt while trying to remove it without breaking the kiss. His mouth was doing wicked things to mine, and I didn't want it to stop. Unfortunately, he had to though. Grayson broke from the kiss long enough to remove his shirt, but he didn't stop there. While he was at it, he undressed both of us completely and then his warm body was back on top of mine. I moaned into his mouth when his much larger alpha cock pushed up against my smaller one. I couldn't wait to feel him inside me.

"Need you," Grayson said as he kissed his way down my jaw and neck. When he got to my collarbone, he gave it a little nibble and I groaned loudly. Sure, we were outside, but there was nobody around except the critters that lived near the lake.

"Grayson. Take me. Please. I want to be yours," I said as I grabbed my mate's hair and yanked his head up until his gaze met mine. I quickly found myself flipped over onto my stomach and then my mate was between my cheeks. With the first swipe of his tongue, I groaned and he moaned.

"So good. So sweet yet still a little spicy, just like your scent. I'll never get enough of you, mate, so be prepared for this for the rest of our lives," Grayson said before he thrust his tongue into my ready hole. I ached with need, and by the time Grayson had cleaned up all of the slick that had leaked everywhere, I was ready to burst.

"Grayson, gonna cum just as soon as you enter me. Please, I ache. Want you. Need your knot. Please, alpha. Claim me." I rambled on and on, and finally, Grayson pulled his mouth away and got up on his knees behind me. When he pulled me up onto my knees as well, I didn't know what to expect at first. I got my answer when he quickly turned my head and thrust his tongue back in my mouth.

Grayson pushed me down onto my side on the daybed and covered my body with his, never once breaking the kiss. When I felt his cock probing at my slick entrance, I moved my right leg forward a little to give him more room. It was exactly what he needed because the head of his thick cock popped through my hole, and I shouted as my own member started throbbing with what I knew would be my first of many orgasms.

"Grayson! Ungh!" I shouted as I reached over, and after getting a good grip on his ass, I yanked my mate into me as hard as I could.

"Shit! Jai! No!" It was too late though. I felt Grayson's knot starting to swell, and I tried my best to roll onto my back so I was facing my mate. "So sorry. I can't stop." Grayson said just before he yanked out of me, and after pushing me to my back, he grabbed my legs and thrust back into me in one quick, hard thrust. He continued to thrust as hard and fast as he could, his inflating knot adding to my pleasure, and I let him know by moaning as loud as I could.

"Mine," I said as my cock started spurting another release on my stomach and chest. At the same time, my channel clamped down on Grayson's cock, and with one final thrust that bordered on painful, he pushed his knot all the way into my body and he stuck there. I felt his knot swell larger than I anticipated, but it caused me to spew even more release between us. Grayson leaned down and growled at me again.

"Mine. My mate," he said just before he sunk his canines into my neck where it and my shoulder met. Instinct took over, and I found the same spot on him and claimed him as my mate, as well. When I did, I felt a sudden burst of warmth inside my channel, and Grayson screamed into my neck where his canines were still buried. We both quickly pulled away and licked the bites clean. They rapidly healed leaving behind our claiming bites.

I looked up into my mate's eyes and smiled, happy and content while he was knotted inside me. He kissed me gently and wrapped his arms around my shoulders and buried his face in my neck and started nibbling and licking my overly sensitive claiming bite. I moaned into the night and he chuckled.

"You like that, huh? I love you, Jai. Thank you for putting up with my ass."

"Mmm, you have such a nice ass. Why wouldn't I? I love you too, mate. All mine. I promise to be a good mate. We're in this together, and I can't wait to spend the rest of my life beside you, wrapped up in your arms."

I moaned again as his cock twitched, and Grayson thrust down, pushing his knot against my prostate. I kept moaning, and when I was writhing beneath my mate, he took mercy on me and wrapped a strong hand around my throbbing cock and stroked it until I spilled between us once again.

When I was flooded with Grayson's thoughts and memories, the last thing I remember was a very recent thought of how he felt about me, and his worry about being a good enough protector and provider. I wanted to reassure my alpha, my mate, but as my bà had warned, my body immediately flushed, and my mating heat overtook me.

Grayson — 9

If the previous four days were a glimpse of the future, I was certainly looking forward to when my mate went into heat again and again. My biggest concern would be our kids though. If subsequent ones were this intense, we'd need someone to watch over our kids for us.

When I wasn't knotted to him, he was either begging me to pound into him, or he was busy riding me. He looked so beautiful on top of me while delirious with his mating heat. Thankfully, he pulled away from me yesterday afternoon and had been asleep since. I collapsed beside him and joined him in exhausted slumber.

But now that he'd been asleep for well over twelve hours, my bear was pushing me to feed our mate. I'd gotten up several times and cleaned my feisty mate up as best as I could, but he would still need a shower. After so many days spent in bed, the shower I'd taken had felt amazing. But Jai's shower would have to wait. I needed to feed him. I grabbed a pair of sweats I'd retrieved from my truck and pulled them on.

When I checked on Jai through our bond, I found him to still be in a deep sleep, so I went down to his well-stocked kitchen and pulled out the items I'd need to make him lunch. Once I'd fixed a meal that made my bear happy, I put everything on a tray I'd found in the pantry and went back to my slumbering mate.

I know he needed sleep, but I was starting to get worried. After setting the tray down on a chair in the massive master bedroom, I crawled back into bed and started nuzzling and kissing Jai's neck. I'd discovered it was one of his favorite things, and I made sure to do it as often as I remembered. He moaned when I got to his claiming bite, and when I gave it a gentle suck, his arms snaked around my neck and held me tight.

"Good afternoon, mate. It's time to eat. I'd let you sleep, but my bear is grouchy and is insisting that I feed you."

"Mmm food. Food good," Jai moaned into my neck, but then all of a sudden he froze before he shoved me away.

"Mate? You claimed me? I'm really your mate?"

Shit. I was positive Jai was there with me and was coherent enough when we claimed each other. As I searched my memories, I quickly found myself flat on my back with my naked mate on top of me. His lips crashed to mine, and when he thrust his tongue in, I moaned.

"Yes, I was coherent. I'm just so happy to have a mate. And I thought for a moment that I dreamt it all. I've longed for a mate for so long."

"Mmm," I replied to Jai's answer though our bond. I needed to stop my feisty mate though. He needed to eat. "Sweetheart, we need to get you fed first. You've had nothing but protein bars, granola bars, energy drinks, and water for the past four days. Please, you need to eat."

Jai pulled back and sat up on my lap and stared down at me. "I've been warned about this. You alphas seem to have a thing about feeding your pregnant mates."

I gasped at what he'd said. I couldn't yet hear a heartbeat other than his. But that didn't mean that Jai didn't already know. After all, he was the one that would be carrying our child.

"Are you sure?" I asked as I gently cupped his stomach. He swatted my hands away and glared at me. I raised an eyebrow in question, and he relented and smiled.

"I'm not sure. I feel different. But that might be the fact that you claimed me, and I sense you through our mating bond. Let me go to the bathroom, and whatever you've fixed over there smells heavenly, so I certainly want some of it."

"It's steak," I said as I chuckled at Jai's expression.

"Hmm. I wouldn't have thought that. I guess my sniffer is off a bit. Maybe I am pregnant after all. Should we schedule an appointment with Arik?"

"Even if you aren't pregnant, and honestly, I can't see how you aren't, we should still schedule an appointment with Arik."

Jai nodded then got up and sort of hobbled towards the bathroom. Yeah, I did that. My bear was preening, and I couldn't blame him. Jai had such a nice ass. It was firm and my cock looked amazing thrusting…

"I can hear you, Grayson. Tell me, have you always been this naughty?"

"Shit. How do I turn this off?"

"Please don't. I'd hate it if you cut me off from our mate bond."

"What? No! That's not what I meant! I just wanted to figure out how to not project every thought to you. I would never completely shut you off. I could never hurt you that way."

"We can talk about it over lunch. My bà had many conversations with all of us about how the mate bond worked. Hopefully, what he passed on to me will work for you."

I heard water running in the bathroom so I assumed Jai was washing his hands. He stepped out of the bathroom just moments later and walked directly back to me and climbed back on my lap.

"I thought you said you would eat just as soon as you went to the bathroom?"

"I should have known you'd remember that. Alright. Should I get dressed first?"

"Are you planning on showering right after we eat?"

"Are you saying I stink?"

"Sweetheart, I'd never say that. But I will remind you that you are still covered in sweat, cum, slick, and saliva. You sure you don't want to shower?"

"Oh my god. How can you stand the smell of me?" Jai asked as he climbed off of me. I grabbed him around the waist and swung him up in my arms. After striding to the loveseat in the room, I sat him down and then retrieved the tray that had his now lukewarm lunch on it.

"Where's yours?"

"Downstairs in the microwave. I figured I'd feed you first and then I'd go down and eat mine while you were in the shower."

"Nope. No way," Jai said as he got up and carried his tray out the bedroom door. I quickly followed, still admiring his bare behind. He must have known what I was doing because he gave it a quick shake before he continued down the stairs. I chuckled at my mate. He really was feisty, and I was certainly going to enjoy having him by my side.

Jai didn't stop until he got to the kitchen, and when he placed his tray down on the table, I retrieved my plate from the microwave and joined him.

"It's not that I don't appreciate you bringing me lunch in bed. That was so sweet and romantic, and I can't wait to thank you for that later. But there's no reason for you to not eat when I do."

"I just want to take care of you."

"And you have. Beautifully. Now, eat so we can get to dessert."

"I didn't make dessert. Should I find something really quick?" I started to get up, but the image Jai sent me through our mate bond had my dick going to full-mast, and my ass returning to the chair. Apparently, I was dessert, and he was going to enjoy me while we showered. Together. I'd never showered with anyone before, but I was looking forward to showering with Jai. Especially if he got dirty before getting clean.

"Are you sure your as old as you are? Because I'd swear you were a teenager," I said as I cut into my steak.

"Yep, I'm actually a very old man. I'm sorry you got me for a mate."

"What? Why? Eat." He wasn't eating and I started to sense despair from my mate. That just wouldn't do.

"I'm closer to two hundred fifty than I am two hundred."

"Does it bother you that I'm so young then? Perhaps you wanted a more mature mate?"

"Fuck that. I want someone…." Jai blushed bright red and trailed off his comment. It didn't matter though. When we claimed each other, I saw all Jai's desires, and I had every intention of fulfilling them. I was young and shouldn't have any issues when it came to stamina.

"I know exactly what you want, mate. And I have every intention of giving it to you. As well as fulfilling each and every one of your fantasies. But for now, eat." I did my best to give Jai a stern look, but it didn't work. He started out chuckling and ended up laughing.

"Okay, sorry. I'm eating. I don't suppose I could meet your bear later, could I?"

"You can, but only if I can meet yours. I'm dying to meet him. I've never met a panda shifter before you. I bet you're just adorable."

"You know, the last thing a man wants is to be considered adorable."

"You sure? Well, too bad. I can't help it. You're adorable. And sexy. And all mine," I growled out, and when Jai's eyes suddenly drooped, I knew I'd made my point.

"Okay. I take it back. You can find me adorable."

"Good. Because you are." We ate the rest of our food, and when we got up to take the plates to the kitchen, I remembered my earlier conversation with Ryker.

"Oh, hey, I almost forgot. I called Ryker earlier, and he said congratulations and that we should plan on taking the rest of the week off."

"The rest of the week? What day is it?"

"Friday."

"Friday?" Jai shouted as he put his plate in the dishwasher.

"Yeah, I claimed you on Monday evening, and you went into heat. You were in heat until yesterday afternoon. You slept all of last night and this morning."

"Why didn't you wake me?"

"Because you needed sleep. You needed to recuperate. I slept on and off, but mostly, I just laid there with you in my arms. Did you know, I absolutely love having you in my arms. Do you by chance like to cuddle? I would love to hold you in my arms on the back deck and look at the stars."

"That sounds heavenly. I love to cuddle. We could go do that now."

"Sweetheart, you haven't looked outside yet, have you?"

"What? No. Why?" Jai asked as he hurried to the back windows.

"Snow! It snowed already? It's only September!"

"True. But it's the end of September, and it's supposed to only be here until early next week."

"Let me guess, your bear is dying to go out in the snow and play."

"He'll survive. He's seen plenty of snow before. I thought pandas were supposed to like snow, as well."

"I never said my bear didn't like snow. It's just much more obvious for you. You're an arctic bear; I'm an Asian bear. Difference."

"Yes, there is. And when I introduce you to my bear later on, he'll get to play in the snow."

"Oh, that sounds like fun. When you talked to Ryker earlier, did he mention anything else about Harvey?"

"Yeah, he said Edison told him Harvey didn't make it back to his den's camp. But we knew that would be the outcome with him. His dad is supposed to start down this way, looking for his son, sometime around the end of next week. He'll be here shortly after."

"Is that when the attack is coming?"

"He didn't say. We'll be okay to go outside, but we can't wander far from the cabin. Not that being inside would protect us."

"Edison put a protection spell on my cabin. I can show you how far out it goes, but I think Ryker is probably first in line for attack."

"Maybe, but he has Arin, and he might not be perfect every time, but there's nothing meek about his powers."

"Yeah, I guess I forgot about that. And it's not like Edison would ever let anything happen to one of his children. That man is seriously intimidating."

"True. So I believe you mentioned something about a shower?"

Jai's eyes heated again, and he took off running for the stairs. I quickly followed because I had a mate to catch.

Jai — 10

We didn't quite make it to the bathroom before Grayson ended up knotted inside me again. Once his knot went down enough to release from my body, he picked me up and carried me to the bathroom and into the shower. I was certainly not going to complain.

After our shower, we quickly dried off, but didn't bother getting dressed.

"Okay, so since I've never seen a panda shifter before, I think you should go first."

"Oh, you do, do you? What if I wanted to see your polar bear first?"

"Then I'd shift for you and show you. But you've seen a polar bear before, I know you've seen Troy shifted."

"True. But Troy isn't my mate."

"Alright. Let's go. I don't want you outside without being shifted for too long. It's cold and well, we're naked."

"Such a good mate you are. Are you always going to be so worried about my comfort?"

"I can't help it, Jai. It's just part of who I am. I need to know that you are safe and well cared for. Come on, I'll shift for you so you can meet my bear. He's more than ready to sniff around you."

I didn't get a chance to tell Grayson I was only joking around with him, that I didn't mind shifting first. He simply walked out onto the back deck and then hopped off. I was going to have to yell at him about that. My back deck was elevated to what would amount to a second story balcony. I rushed to the edge, and when I looked over, I was met by the sight of my mate's large and intimidating bear.

"Don't even think it. You take the stairs."

"We're going to have a talk about that little stunt you just pulled, mate." I replied as I quickly walked down the stairs. Grayson must have swept them off at some point because the snow was gone from them. By the time I reached the ground, I was face to chest with a very furry and warm looking Grayson.

"Oh wow. You're huge!" I said, stating the obvious as I ran my fingers though his thick, coarse hair. I'd seen Troy shifted before, but I'd never gotten this close or touched him. I took a step back when Grayson brought his head down to my level and started sniffing first my neck where my claim bite was and then my stomach.

"Smell something you like, big guy? Yeah, if you can smell it, then you should know that you put that cub in there." I gently grabbed his ears and gave them a quick rub before I took a step back and shifted with my mate. I was tiny compared to Grayson's much larger bear, but I knew I'd never have anything to fear from him. He was my mate and would always protect me.

"Okay, I stand by my earlier statement. You're simply adorable," Grayson said as he ran his now human hands through my own thick fur. "I love the mask you have on your eyes. Maybe I should call you bandit instead of sweetheart?"

"Do and I'll tie you to the bed."

"Oh! Kinky! I like it. Is that what you want? Does my adorable mate want to tie me to the bed and have his way with me?"

I sent images of that exact scenario to Grayson whose eyes instantly heated, but I took off at a run towards the woods instead of going upstairs like I really wanted to. I was quickly overtaken by my very large and powerful mate who gently tagged me with a massive paw. His bear was so much larger than mine that it wasn't difficult for him to get me to stop. Once I did, I simply rolled over and presented my belly to him. His bear instantly sniffed all over me and let out a loud grunt when he got to my lower abdomen again.

"Can you smell a baby, Grayson?"

"Yes. We need to get you to Arik though. I want to make sure you're as well taken care of as possible, so when we get back, let's give him a call and set up an appointment for you."

I internally groaned because there was no way I'd let Grayson know I was both dreading and looking forward to his over protectiveness in the upcoming months. I remembered how crazy Troy and Ryker were with their mates when they were pregnant. My mate didn't appear that he would be any different.

We spent the afternoon walking around in the woods that surrounded the cabin. It gave Grayson an opportunity to get to know the area as well as mark his territory. I was proud to have such a protective mate and was relieved and excited that he was anxious to mark the area as his.

"You ready to head back to the cabin? It's getting dark, and although I'm not worried about it, we should probably figure out dinner as well as give Arik a call. I also want to check in with War and see if he had any new information regarding Hank and his gang."

"We can go back whenever you want. I'm more than ready to soak in the tub and just relax," I said.

"Why didn't you say you were tired?"

"I didn't say I was tired. I just said I was ready to relax, that's all. I think the past week has caught up with me. I'm ready to rest.

And I'm telling you now. I know you'll fuss over me if I don't so I wanted you to know."

Grayson's bear let out a low, grumbling growl, and he took off towards the cabin. I trotted behind him and in no time, we were at the base of the steps that led up to the back deck. We quickly shifted and climbed the stairs that would lead to the door we'd exited several hours ago.

"Wow, I didn't realize we'd been out so long. It's already dinnertime. Can your bath hold off until after? Or do you want to soak now while I fix something to eat?"

"Actually, I want to grab some sweats and a shirt and then I'd love to fix something with you. You don't always have to be the one to cook, you know."

"I realize that, sweetheart. I just like doing things for you."

"And I appreciate it, Grayson. But there will be times that I want to do things for you, too. I want to cook with you, okay?" I asked as I wrapped my arms around his waist and rested my head on his chest. I was interested in seeing what my mate looked like in a few more years. He was still so very young and his muscular build hadn't yet completely filled out. Sure, there were shifters that never got as bulky as Troy; Ryker was one of them. But I had a feeling that my baby alpha was just getting warmed up.

"Whatcha thinking about there, sweetheart?"

"Mmm, you. In say, five years."

"Oh, yeah? And what about me in five years?"

"I was wondering how much more muscular you were going to end up being. I mean, Ivan is certainly broader than you."

"He is. Dad's side of the family are all huge. Da's side are more compact. I think I'm a good combination of the two."

"Yep, I have to agree. Come on. Let's get some clothes on and then we'll find something to eat. Then maybe I can convince you to soak in the tub with me?"

"Well, since I know you have a gigantic tub, I know there's room. I'd love nothing more than to hold you while we relax in the tub." Grayson gave me a swift kiss before we walked off towards the stairs to head back to our room. I needed to talk to him about moving the rest of his things in. Maybe he'd be willing to pick up his stuff tomorrow?

After we quickly pulled on sweats and T-shirts, we made dinner that consisted of spaghetti, salad, and garlic bread from the freezer. I was going to have to up my game though, because I thought I'd made more than enough food, but everything was eaten quickly. It had been so long since I'd been around a young alpha that I'd forgotten how much they actually eat. Sure, Troy and Ryker ate a lot, but not nearly as much as my mate.

"Hey, question for you," I said as I turned over in the bathtub and laid on Grayson's chest. I started drawing circles around his left nipple which quickly pebbled at my touch. Interesting.

"Hmm?"

"So the beginning of the week it was mentioned about you moving in here with me, and I was wondering if you'd still be willing to do that? I'm not really looking for a part-time mate, and I really don't know where we'd put all of my stuff in that little cabin of yours."

"Sweetheart, my truck is full of my stuff. I have maybe two boxes and a small bag of clothes and things at the cabin. I just didn't unload the truck because I didn't know where to put my things."

"Grayson, I want you to feel that this is your home, too. You don't need my permission to place your things somewhere. You're more than welcome to put them wherever. I want you to add all of your things to the house. I want to go out and get new things with you and make changes to the house. If there's something you really don't care for, please speak up and let me know. I can't get rid of something if I don't know you don't like it."

"From what I've seen so far, there's nothing wrong anywhere in your house."

"No. See, you're missing the point. It's not my house. It became ours the second you claimed me. Everything that I have is equally yours. I want to share everything with you." I sat up and straddled Grayson's lap and looked at him. It was going to take some time, but I knew he'd eventually feel completely comfortable here. He was already trying, and that was a huge step.

"Okay. So it's our house. Does that mean we can maybe find some drawer space for my clothes? I figured I'd be living out of boxes for a while."

"We don't need to find you space. I have a completely empty dresser that you can have. And your uniforms and shirts can hang on the other side of the closet. Half of it's empty. I've never given up hope that I'd one day find my mate. Now, here you are. We just have to get you moved in." Grayson gave me a huge smile, and I felt the happiness radiating from him. That made both me and my bear happy.

"I'm getting great happiness from you. What's up?"

"I'm just happy. I'm in my mate's arms, in the bath, and if we're to believe your bear, we're pregnant and will be welcoming a cub of our own in five months. What more could I want?"

"I really like all of that. Thank you, sweetheart, for giving me a chance. I really was an ass to you and I'm sorry. I want to make you happy. Not just because you're my mate, either. You're a wonderful person, and you deserve so much. If I can do something to put a smile on your face, I consider it a win and well worth any effort."

"You were? When?" I asked, jokingly. When we got into a tickle match in the tub, water went everywhere but, in the end, I won when I started sucking on Grayson's claiming bite, and he moaned as he grabbed my ass. He somehow managed to pick us both up and get us dried off and into bed without me having to stop my exploration of his body with my mouth.

Grayson — 11

Jai was definitely pregnant. Even if the morning sickness wasn't a dead giveaway, we could both hear the heartbeat two days after his heat ended. That was several weeks ago. We'd called Alpha War to talk to Alpha Mate Arik, but the call forwarded to Troy because Arik was in heat. So our little cub would have a den mate, or mates, with a birthday close to his or hers.

When Jai wasn't worshipping the toilet, he was trying his best to be cheerful for me. I did everything I could for him, but I was at a complete loss. I'd been around Da when he was pregnant with Cassie, but I was four. I didn't remember much.

"Jai, sweetheart, please. Let me call and ask for help. You're not keeping anything down anymore. Barely even water. I'm really getting worried."

"Okay. Call Troy and ask him to send Edison. Edison can help."

"You sure?" I asked as I ran a cool rag along the back of Jai's neck. It helped, a little. I was willing to do anything to help at this point. Jai nodded and then laid down on the cool tile of the bathroom floor.

"Okay. I'll go grab my phone and be right back."

My poor mate was exhausted though. He was asleep by the time I got up from the floor to grab my phone. Any chance he got to nap in between bouts of sickness, I was all for. I tapped the screen to connect the call as I walked back to the bathroom. Jai was still napping so I stood just outside the door so I wouldn't disturb him. Troy must have been busy, because he picked up just as I was about to hang up. But he did have triplets, so he was busy all the time, even with Elliot as his mate.

"Hey, Grayson. Everything okay?"

"Troy, I need help. Actually, Jai needs help. He's really sick. He can't even keep down water, and I'm not sure what to do. He's sleeping in the bathroom on the floor right now. He told me to call you and ask for Edison. I'm really worried, Troy. His mind is fuzzy through our bond, and his heartbeat is really low."

"Grayson, don't worry. I'm hanging up now and sending Edison over immediately. Don't worry. Edison will take care of Jai, and I'm sure Wallace will be there for you. Just do what they say because they really do know what they're doing."

"I will. Thanks, Troy. I'll be back at work just as soon as I can. I never expected Jai to get so sick."

"Don't worry about it. It happens. Arik is puking like crazy again. War's beside himself, too. He's proud, but also worried. We've all been there. Let me go so I can get in contact with Edison."

"Thanks, again, Troy." I hung up, and before I could even put the phone back on the night stand, Edison and Wallace appeared in the bedroom with me.

"Okay, that's just creepy."

"We're sorry, Grayson. We were unsure if you'd like for us to knock or ring the bell so in we came. Now, do you want to move your mate to the bed, or shall I?"

"He growls whenever I try to pick him up. He says it upsets his stomach. I'm really worried, Edison. He's almost a month pregnant, and we have another month of this? I'm not going to make it. His heartrate is low which concerns me more than the fact that he can't even keep down water."

"Alright. I promise, I'll take good care of him. But next time, don't wait so long to call for help. He'll be feeling much better tomorrow, but for now, I'll get him in bed and settled, and Wallace will take you downstairs and take care of you. When was the last time you ate, Grayson?"

"Umm..."

"Come on, Grayson. I've been told I'm an excellent cook, so let's see what we can find in the kitchen," Wallace said as he wrapped his hand around my bicep and pulled me from the room. I knew I needed to go, but I didn't want to leave my mate. Neither did my bear, but Wallace was insistent so I went with him. When I turned and looked through the doorway, Edison had Jai in bed, and he looked more peaceful than he had in weeks.

I'd failed my mate. I couldn't even take care of him properly. Now Wallace had to take care of me? Really not one of my better moments. I followed Wallace down to the kitchen where he immediately made himself at home and started rummaging through the fridge and the pantry. He must have known exactly what he wanted because he came out of the pantry with both arms full of items.

"Do you need help?"

"Nope. I've got it. When you're as old as I am, you've pretty much figured out how to do certain things. And I've figured out cooking. Have a seat. We'll have a conversation while I throw this stuff together."

"Sure. What is it you're making?"

"Well, for Jai, I'm making chicken and rice soup. It'll be good for his stomach, and he should be able to keep it down. Especially after a little help from Edison. For the rest of us, I'll add several more vegetables and a thickener, and it'll be a chicken stew."

"What's Edison doing to Jai? Is he okay?"

"Hang on." Wallace stared off into the room, and when a slow smile spread on his face, he looked at me and nodded. "Yes, Jai is just fine. He's dehydrated, as you'd said, but he's just fine. So is the baby."

It was such a relief to hear that my mate and our baby were going to be okay. I was really worried, and my bear was driving me crazy about the fact that our mate wasn't able to keep anything down. My relief must have been apparent because Wallace came over to the other side of the island and wrapped his arm around my shoulders and gave me a tight squeeze.

"Grayson, it's okay to ask for help. Not only are you young, but everyone in the den knows that the way Ivan raised you and your siblings was much more traditional; and honestly, that makes things difficult. There's no shame in asking for help, nor is there in asking for advice. Did you know that when I met Edison, I was of course enamored with my mate, but I was also terrified? I was a lot like you were. I didn't know much about being a mate, and I sure didn't know anything about raising babies. But like so many, we got pregnant when I claimed Edison. And we had a beautiful son three months later. Thankfully, for me, and Edison as well as Arthur, we lived in the coven. There were other warlocks there that knew what to do and how to take care of Edison. Warlocks cannot give birth without the assistance of another warlock, so I could have easily lost both of them if we were anywhere else. But the point is, I had help, and I still didn't know what to do. So don't feel bad, or less-than, if you ask for assistance. That's what dens do. Well, that's what they're supposed to do."

I thought about everything Wallace said to me as he walked back to the other side of the island and started cutting up chicken and adding it to a pot. Then he added water and a little salt and pepper and that was it. "Do you know if Jai has a rice cooker, or not?"

"Yeah, it's right here," I said as I got off the stool and went to the cabinet on the other side of the kitchen and pulled it out. Jai had everything we'd ever need for the kitchen and thankfully, I'd discovered where most things were over the past several weeks.

"Thanks. Do you want to start the rice while I get another cutting board and cut up the vegetables?"

"Sure." I didn't really know what to say. Wallace had given me so much to think about, and it was going to take some time to process it. "Hey, Wallace?"

"Yes? What's up, Grayson?"

"Honestly, I'm not sure. I think I'm a little overwhelmed. Before Jai and I claimed each other, Edison talked to me and told me to not let our ages be an issue."

"That's wise advice. Edison is almost a thousand years old, and I haven't quite hit eight hundred yet. That was a lot to take in at first. But I didn't let it get to me, my mate said things worked out for a reason. We've had almost six hundred years together, and they've been amazing."

"Can I ask a personal question?"

"Of course, we're pretty much an open book."

"Well, the twins are only twenty-nine. Is it normal to have children so far apart or after so long together?"

"No, on both counts. And it's no secret that the pregnancy with the twins was very difficult on Edison. Arthur was an extreme help with their birth. But for whatever reason, the fates decided we were meant to have the twins. We were surprised when Edison had a fertile period when he got pregnant with Elliot. It had been a couple hundred years since he'd had one. Then, after he got pregnant with the twins, he hasn't had one since. When Jai's meant to stop having children, his heat cycles will end. That's just the way fate is. You have to trust that they know what's best for you and your mate."

Wallace added the vegetables to a second pot and then loaded the dishes in the dishwasher. I watched him, and he appeared so at ease and at home. As far as I knew, he'd never been to the house before.

"Wallace?" He was smiling when he turned to look at me. I tried to not let it get to me because I was sure he knew it was coming.

"Yes?"

"Did it bother you to move in with Edison when you two mated?"

"No. It was where he needed to be. He had everything he needed at the coven. He needed to be around other warlocks, and I had no pride to speak of. Aside from the ages, you remind me a lot of myself at the beginning of our mating."

"How did you two meet? Do you mind I'm asking?"

"Nope, I don't mind. We met because the fates told Edison to go to Scotland and find me. So, he did. I'd been hiding and living in the Highlands for a long time by then. Back then, we were hunted and murdered even more than we would be today. My parents were killed when I was still in my teens. One day, my da came home from the market and told my mum and I to run and hide in the Highlands. Mum wouldn't leave Da, but they somehow convinced me to leave and hide. As soon as I was out of the village, I shifted and took off. I was lucky enough to be able to find a cave to make home and lived off the land for several decades. Then one day when I'd just returned from hunting, there was the most beautiful man I'd ever seen sitting in my cave in front of the fire."

"And he tried to claim me, then and there, on the cave floor," Edison said from behind me. I whipped around to stare at the warlock who had a habit of sneaking up on people.

"Not my most shining moment, no," Wallace said before he started laughing.

"Is Jai okay?"

"Yes, your mate is just fine. He's sleeping peacefully and will remain that way for another hour or so."

"Does that mean you *helped* him?"

"That's exactly what it means. He'll need to drink the tea I'll give you for him, several times a day. It will help calm his stomach, and he'll be able to keep down the water and food he needs. This should only last but a month longer and then he'll feel better. Arik is just as sick, but because he's drinking the tea, he's able to keep down fluids and small amounts of food. Jai will tell you what his stomach can handle and what it can't. Don't fight him on it. I know your bear is going to push you to force him to eat, but he'll be fine. Promise."

"And the baby?"

"The baby is just fine."

"That's a relief. I've been so worried. I tried to help, and I thought about calling Da, but Jai and him, I don't know; I think maybe Jai doesn't care for my omega father."

"I'm sure that's not the case. But taking him to dinner at your parents' before you actually claimed him might have been something he wasn't expecting," Edison said.

"Oh! Yeah, you're probably right."

"Grayson, next time, call sooner."

"Yes, sir, I will. I think I need to take Ryker and Troy up on their offer to answer any questions I have."

"Any of us alphas would gladly answer any questions you have, Grayson. All you have to do is ask. We've all been there, me especially. Well, except maybe Gage, he's a little absent-minded."

"Thanks, Wallace. Do you mind if I go up and sit with Jai? Would that be okay?"

"That's fine. I'm sure your bear wants to see your mate so go on up. Wallace and I will bring you two supper in just a little while."

"Thanks, Edison." I got up and quickly made my way back to our bedroom. Edison was right, I needed to see my mate and be sure he was okay.

Jai — 12

I was feeling so much better. And when I opened my eyes, there was my handsome mate, sleeping beside me. Edison and Wallace were sitting on the loveseat in the room. Nope, that wasn't creepy at all. I started to ask them what they were doing there, but Edison put his finger over his lips to let me know not to talk. I nodded, but when I went to get up to use the bathroom, Grayson's arm shot out and cinched around me.

"Hey, I just gotta pee," I said quietly.

"Sorry. I didn't realize you were awake and thought you were falling out of bed or something. I don't know. My brain is fuzzy."

After getting up and taking care of business in the bathroom, I realized my stomach was feeling a whole lot calmer, and I actually wanted something to drink. I washed my hands and went to go find some water, but instead, I was met by a smiling Wallace who was holding a tray with a glass of water that looked refreshing and a bowl of soup.

"Sit and you can eat. Edison said you should be able to keep both the water and the soup down. He's downstairs with Grayson, showing him how to make your tea."

"Is that the stuff that Troy said smells terrible, but helped Elliot?"

"That would be the stuff, yes. You'll have to drink it three times a day, at least. More if you're feeling sick. But it will help. And I'm told that Elliot says you get used to the flavor."

"Thank you," I said as I climbed back in the bed. I noticed the sheets smelled clean and fresh, and I wondered if I had Edison to thank for that, as well. I had just sat the glass of cool water back on the tray when Grayson came in with his own tray.

"Hey, sweetheart. You're looking so much better. How are you feeling?"

"Like I got hit by a moving vehicle. I'm so tired, and my entire body feels heavy. It's like my arms and legs weigh a ton each."

"That'll pass. That's just the effects of the help I gave you earlier. But don't worry, you and the baby are perfectly fine."

"Thank you, Edison. I really tried to keep water and crackers down, but the past few days, it's gotten so much worse."

"It'll be hit or miss. You never know if you'll spend a lot of time throwing up, or if you'll be just fine. Each pregnancy will be different so don't expect this one to be the same as the next," Edison told me.

"Noted. Well, I hope to have many more cubs with my mate, so I guess, we'll have to wait and see."

"That's a good plan. You two eat your dinner, and Wallace and I will be downstairs in the kitchen if you need us. Take your time and give a shout when you're finished."

"Thanks, for everything," Grayson said and I nodded in agreement. My mate gave me a quick kiss before he sat a cup of what could only be my tea on my tray.

"I know it smells like wet, smelly socks, but I'm told it will calm your stomach."

"You know, you'd think with as powerful as he is, he'd be able to make the tea smell and taste better."

"I think it's the things that are in it. I'm sorry, sweetheart. But it will help, so please drink."

"I will. Don't worry. I want to be able to walk and sit upright without puking."

"I'm so sorry."

"Don't start. We want our cub. You were so excited about it when you found out I was pregnant, and I need you to not be sorry. This is just part of it."

"I know, however, that doesn't make it any easier. Can you try a little bit of the soup? Yours is a very basic chicken and rice. I was told it would probably be a good idea to keep the ingredients on hand for the next month or so."

"I'm sure. I've always loved chicken and rice soup. I remember my bà making it for me when I was a little kid so it's always been one of my favorites."

"That's convenient then. Can you try, please?"

"Yes, tell your bear to not worry. I'm eating."

"Thank you, I can't help it. I love you so much, and it hurts when I see you in agony. Do you remember sleeping on the bathroom floor for the past two days?"

"What? No." Grayson shared his memories of a very sick me the past several weeks. Apparently, as soon as we both heard our cub's heartbeat, I started getting sick. It was just in the mornings at first, but it steadily progressed to an all day and night thing. "Wow. I'm sorry. I never meant to worry you so much, alpha."

"Hey, it's alright. I'm always going to worry about you. Once you start feeling a little better, maybe we can go back to work? That'll help you feel better, I'm sure."

"Yeah, about that, what if I wanted to take some time off? I know you're really worried about finances and everything, but I've had well over a century to save."

"I'm getting there. Just bear with me. Wallace told me that eventually it wouldn't bother me that you were the more established mate. It really helped when he told me about how he and Edison met. But if you want to take time off, I'm all for it."

"Really?" I asked, excited about the prospect of staying home and raising a house full of kids with my mate. I know he wanted to work, and I was okay with that. But I was an omega, and I yearned for cubs of my own.

"Yes, sweetheart, really. Ryker and Troy have been quite understanding. But with Arik pregnant, and Harrison and Bradley into everything, Troy has been handling a lot of the den stuff. I know that Ryker could use my help, so I want to go back when you're feeling better.

"Well, maybe we can compromise? How about, in a few days, you drop me off at War and Arik's place and then go into work. I know you'd feel better getting back to more of a routine, and I'll hang out with Arik. Edison and Wallace will be nearby to help if needed, and your bear will feel better with me closer to Edison, I'm sure. It's been over a month since you faced-off with Harvey. Surely there's news about that?"

"I haven't asked. I've been most concerned about you and the baby. But you're right, I would feel much better with you there instead of here, alone. I know we have our bond and can always communicate like that, but if you're closer to Edison, my bear and I would be much happier. We can ask if you'd like."

"I would, yes."

Grayson gave me a quick kiss on the cheek before he spooned another bite of chicken stew into his mouth. I realized that in all of the memories he'd shared with me he didn't show how he'd taken care of himself, only me. I was sure he was both hungry as well as exhausted. He looked tired, and I knew that as shifters, we tended to have great endurance. But my mate *looked* tired, which meant he was near exhaustion, which was a big deal for an alpha as young as him.

"Grayson, when was the last time you ate something? Something other than a protein bar?" My baby alpha blushed and looked down at his stew like it had become super interesting to him. "Grayson, please look at me." When he did, he had what could only be described as a guilty look on his face.

"I was more worried about you than me. I haven't been able to go to the store this week, and we ran out of protein bars last week."

"So what have you eaten this week?" I asked. I was about to flip my lid at my mate. He needed to take care of himself and not just worry about me.

"I ate the fruit we had. I really need to make a grocery run. We have food, but what's left needs to be cooked. The things that are quick and easy are gone."

I groaned in frustration. My poor mate, he'd practically starved himself to take care of me. "Grayson, baby, don't do that. You have to take care of yourself, too."

"It's not the first time I've gone without. You know it took us weeks to get here from Alaska. We had to be careful because polar bears aren't found this far inland or south. There wasn't a lot to hunt."

"Okay, you're going to make me cry so let's pick a happier topic. I hate what happened to all of you, but I'll forever be grateful to Ivan for getting you all out of there. I just don't understand him though."

"Yeah, you and me both. Dad is difficult, to say the least. But on some level, I know he means well. And he's still really young, so there's hope for him. He's only seventy-one, and I hope that means he'll learn something from the other alphas here in the den. I know I have so many questions for them, and they've all told me I could always come to them. I've never had that. Our den was accepting but they weren't open to discussions. They were just, I think Wallace called it traditional. He's right though, it was. Almost to a point that the den suffered for it. But you wanted happier, so let's talk about our cub. I know that makes you happy."

I smiled at Grayson's change of subject. He was correct. Just the thought of our cub made me very happy, indeed. "Yes, it does. Have you thought about how many you want?"

"As many as the fates bless us with. If you're willing, that is. It's always your choice. If you ever don't want me to mate with you during a heat, I know they—"

"Nope, stop right there. I want as many as I can have."

"Sounds good. We have time, but I assumed you'd want the room that's empty to be made into the nursery."

"Yes, that's why I kept it empty. It's closest to us so it's ideal."

"Maybe in a couple months when you're feeling a lot better we can work on it, okay?"

"That works." I looked down and realized that I'd eaten almost every bit of my soup and had drank both my water and my tea. Now I was sleepy and ready to go to bed. Grayson's food was completely gone, and I was sure he could go through a couple more bowls of it. We were interrupted by Wallace knocking on the doorframe, and we both looked up as he entered.

"Good. I see you both ate. Grayson, there's more downstairs, and I know you could use it so we need to get you another bowl, or two. Also, War is here and he'd like to talk to the two of you for a few minutes if you don't mind."

"No, of course not," I replied as I moved the tray and tried to climb off the bed. Grayson was quickly by my side, and before I could protest, he had me up in his arms and was walking out the door with purpose. "I can walk, you know."

"I do, but this is so much more fun. Besides, I like you right where you are." I smiled and snuggled into my mate's neck and gave him a hasty kiss before I closed my eyes and sighed. It was wonderful to have someone around to care for me. I'd spent so much time alone that I'd forgotten what it was like to be around others.

When we entered the kitchen, our Alpha was sitting at the island with a bowl of stew in front of him.

"I hope you don't mind. Wallace's stew is delicious, though."

"Why would we mind, Alpha?"

"Grayson?"

"Yes, Alpha?"

"When are you ever going to call me War?"

"I don't know if I can do that in your presence."

"Fair enough. You'll get there. Edison asked that I give you an update on the Hank situation."

"I meant to call earlier in the week and ask, but Jai got sicker as the week went on, and I just didn't think."

"And we didn't think to check-in on you. For that, I'm sorry. It won't happen again."

"You've done nothing wrong, Alpha. But you did mention Hank. What do you know?" Grayson asked. He was all business now, and if I wasn't so sick, I'd find it hot. But just the thought of having sex with my mate made my stomach churn. When Grayson chuckled through our mate bond, I realized I'd projected my thoughts to him. Darn it!

"Well, from what Edison has told me, Hank found his son's body last week, and we have only a few days left before his group are here and they attack. So, I'm here to tell you, as your Alpha, I'd feel much better if you two moved into the alpha house until after Hank is dealt with."

Grayson — 13

It was wrong, and I know it was, but I wasn't giving Jai any choice. We were packing a bag and moving into one of the spare rooms at War's house. I wanted Jai closer to Edison, Elliot, and Arin, and they all lived at the alpha house. My mate was grumbling beside me, but I wasn't budging.

"You know I can hear you, right?"

"I know you can. That doesn't bother me. I'm not helpless. I might be an omega but—"

"Don't go there. This has *nothing* to do with you being an omega. I'm not my dad, and I don't share his feelings regarding that. This has *everything* to do with the fact that I love you, I want you safe, and you're pregnant. It would kill me if *anything* happened to you or our cub."

I grabbed my bag and walked out of the bedroom. If I stayed any longer, I'd say something I'd end up regretting. That wasn't uncommon for me, so I needed a moment to calm down.

"Grayson, I'm sorry. You're right and I understand. I've just been on my own for so long."

"Well, you're not alone anymore. If not for me, think about our cub. I don't want anything to happen to either of you. You don't look pregnant, yet, but it doesn't matter. Hank is out to wipe out all male omegas. I'm already a target because I have an omega father which means I must be a deviant. I can't help but want you two safe. I just got you, and I'm not ready to give you up."

"I understand that. And I am sorry."

"Thank you. I'm trying, sweetheart. I'm new to this mate thing so just help me when I mess up, okay. I'm sure I could have done better when it came to telling you we needed to take Alpha up on his offer."

"No, you were fine. I'm done. Be right down."

I heard my mate on the stairs and turned to meet him. He stopped two steps from the bottom and was eye-level with me. After I dropped my bag, I took his and placed it beside mine and then wrapped my arms around him.

"I'm really sorry, Jai. I'll try to approach things differently. I want to always make you happy and keep you safe."

"I know, Grayson, and I'm sorry, too. I'll try to not react so harshly next time. If I have an issue, I'll let you know, but not by throwing a fit."

"Thanks, sweetheart. Come on, we're expected at the alpha house, and I want to get you back in bed soon. You couldn't even sit up, let alone stand, just a few hours ago."

"I know and I'm tired."

"I realize that. You wait here and I'll be back for you. I want to put our bags in the truck and then I'll come back and carry you out."

"You don't have to carry me; I can walk."

"I know, but I like having you near me. And the fact that I can carry you is a bonus."

"Fine, but only because I like it when you carry me."

I smiled at how cute Jai was when he pretended to pout. I picked up both of our bags and quickly took them to Jai's truck in the garage and then rushed back to my rapidly weakening mate and swung him up in my arms.

"You're exhausted. We need to get you into bed, soon."

"I felt fine just a little bit ago, but now my entire body feels weighed down again."

"We'll have you settled in about twenty minutes. If you need to, I can put you in the backseat, and you can lie down."

"No, I can just recline the front one. But you do have to drive."

"I figured as much," I said as I gently placed Jai in the front passenger's seat and then went around to the driver's side. We were on our way to our Alpha's house in no time, and Jai was completely passed out before we even got into Honey Creek. The alpha house was on the other side of our town, about twenty minutes from Jai's cabin on the lake. Well, I guess *our* cabin on the lake. I needed to make plans to have my parents out for dinner. Later.

When I pulled up to the house, there were already several vehicles parked in the drive that weren't normally there. Maybe it would be better if I parked out back by the cabin? Troy came out of the front door with a huge smile on his face.

"I'm glad you two are here. Maybe you can give us a hand with Ivan."

I groaned at the thought of my alpha dad and what he was doing. "What'd he do now?"

"Nothing, really. He's just staring at me, giving me the evil eye. I don't understand. Your dads are fated. He took Sam from our den. Why's he pissed at me?"

"I think it's the whole thing where you helped Da through so many heats. I mean, I just don't understand what else it could be. I know that Jai's had help, but I also know that once he scented me, I was the only one that mattered. Dad would realize that too, if he'd just pull his head out of his ass. It's one of the reasons why he and I just don't seem to get along. And he still punishes Da because of it."

Troy groaned and then looked to the truck and smiled. "I'll get your bags if you get your mate."

"Deal. He's weak again and I'm quite worried. I know he needs lots of rest, and I hope he can get it here."

"He will. Edison will have him resting in no time. Arik is sick again. Although, Edison swears he's only having one this time, Arik doesn't agree."

"He was sick with the twins, right?"

"Yes. Quite. Then he was, umm…yeah. Then he was miserable. So be prepared. That's just how it is. And I've been told it's different with warlocks. They're…yeah, never mind. Let's get Jai settled into your room while you're here. I'm placing you two upstairs, near War and Arik. I figured, with Arik being sick as well, it would be better to have them closer together."

"Sounds good. Thanks, Troy. Let me grab my mate and then I'll go see what I can do about my father."

"Thanks." Troy walked off towards the door, and I gathered Jai into my arms once again. He stirred just a bit when I picked him up, but not much. His poor body was so weak, and it was my fault to some extent. I should have called my da at the beginning of the week. Thankfully, he was there, with a concerned look on his face, when I entered the house.

"Grayson, here, let me show you where Troy put your things, and I'll watch over your mate for a bit."

"You don't have to, Da."

"No, I don't, but I want to. You've run yourself down this week, I've been told. You're no use to your mate if you don't take care of yourself, as well."

"I know." I admitted to myself that Da was right, and I needed to do what I could for Jai. That included making sure I was well enough to care for him, so I needed to listen to my omega father. He'd been pregnant five times, so he knew what Jai was going through. I followed Da's slender body up the stairs and entered a cozy bedroom that had a very soft looking bed against one wall.

"I know Edison has helped with some of the furnishings. Most of the rooms were just empty or had a simple bed in them. I honestly think Edison is hoping to turn the place into a den for shifters that have lost their home den."

"Maybe. We know what that's like," I said as I laid Jai down. He opened his eyes long enough to smile at me and then he sighed and rolled over as I tucked him in. When I stood up, Da was looking at me with a happy and content look on his face.

"Thanks for watching him for me. I want to go talk to Ryker and Troy to see what's going on at work. They're really spread thin with just the two of them. I'm hoping to go back once Jai is stronger."

"You're going to do alright, Grayson. Just hang in there," Da said before patting me on the shoulder and then walking to the other side of the room to pick up the bags and put them on the dresser. "I'm going to go grab my e-reader and then I'll be right back. We're actually on the other end of the hallway, but I won't be gone long."

"It's fine, Da. Jai will probably sleep all night anyway. I won't be gone long. Thanks again," I said as we walked out the door. I went down the stairs, and Da went on to his room at the other end of the hallway. I heard everyone in the kitchen but stopped when the doorbell rang. Wasn't everyone already here?

"Surely they wouldn't ring the bell and expect us to answer. Would they?" Ryker asked.

"No. That's not Hank's style. I'll go see who it is," Troy said as he walked off to the front of the house. I smiled at Arin, who had Edwin in his arms. Their little guy sure was cute.

"Would you like to hold him? You're going to need all the practice you can get soon," Arin asked. He was right; I would. I'd have my own cub soon enough.

"I'd love to, if you and Ryker don't mind."

"He wouldn't have offered if we did, Grayson," Ryker told me as he plucked his son out of his mate's arms and passed him off to me.

"Ryker, it's for you. They said they're your parents. They kinda smell like you so I guess they are?"

"Shit. Did you tell them…"

"Ryker, how nice of you inform us that your child was born." A woman who looked similar to Ryker said with a bit of hopefulness as well as a little disdain.

"Mother, Father, what are you doing here?" I sensed Ryker's distress so I handed Edwin back to his omega father and stood to Ryker's left, Troy on his right, and War came up behind Ryker's parents.

"We came to inspect the child. He or she should have been born by now," his father stated. Inspect the child? Who the hell needed to inspect their grandchild? He was a baby, not a head of lettuce.

"I'm sorry, I believe you said you were here to inspect my child? Who do you two think you are? You left me, on my own, when I was seventeen. Up until then, you basically ignored me and most days you forgot to even feed me dinner. I haven't heard from you in how long? And now that I'm mated, you want to *inspect my child*? I have nothing to say to you two except to get out of here and never return and don't call. You're not welcome here or anywhere near my mate or our children."

"Children? You've had more than one?" His mother asked, looking hopeful. What the hell? Seriously, who were these people?

"Go. Now. You've been warned. Don't come back," Ryker said just before he and Arin disappeared with their little bundle of joy. That was certainly advantageous.

"I believe you heard him. You two really make me wonder how you're his parents," War said from behind them. They looked like they were about to argue until Edison and Wallace appeared beside our Alpha. Yeah, if that trio didn't cause you to pee your pants, there was something wrong with you.

"We're going," Ryker's dad said as he grabbed his mate's arm and pulled her from the room and out the door.

"I don't get them," I said once the door was shut behind them.

"Yeah, most parents are more loving with their cubs. I don't get them either, Grayson," War said with a sad look on his face. It seemed that he was sad for something more than just Ryker's parents being assholes. But what?

"Alright, we have a few things to talk about so let's get to it. Grayson needs to eat again, and then go to bed. He needs to rest for everything that's going to happen tomorrow," Edison said to us.

Tomorrow? Shit just got real.

Jai — 14

I was so warm. I was sleeping on what felt like a cloud, and I could smell my mate. His arms were wrapped around me, and I was certain I could feel a certain part of his anatomy—that I'd not been interested in for the past several weeks—poking me in the small of my back.

"Mmm, sorry, sweetheart. Let me…" Grayson said sleepily as he pulled his hips away from me. That wasn't what I wanted at all. Unfortunately, my stomach still wasn't feeling the greatest and I needed to remember that.

"I'm sorry, Grayson. My stomach just—"

"Don't apologize. I should ask for forgiveness. Let me go get your tea; I'll be right back," Grayson said as he quickly got out of bed. He pulled on a pair of jeans which covered his body from my view. A body I wanted to get to know better. We'd only been together a handful of times before I got sick. I wanted more.

I sat up and when my stomach didn't completely revolt, I tested it again and got out of bed to go to the bathroom. That was my mistake. Walking made me dizzy, which made my stomach roll. I raced to one of the two other doors hoping it was a bathroom and not a closet. It was and I just barely made it to the toilet before the contents of my stomach started coming up.

"On my way, sweetheart. You should have waited for your tea."

I heard Grayson through our bond, and I could tell he was agitated, but I couldn't change what had been done at this point. Grayson came bursting into the bathroom moments later and quickly grabbed a washcloth and wet it for me. I'd finished by then, and he helped me wipe my face and then he placed another cloth on the back of my neck while I quickly brushed my teeth.

"Come on. Let's get you into bed. Da is bringing your tea."

"Thanks. I'm sorry. I just had to pee."

"Did you get to?"

"No, not yet," I replied. Grayson turned me around and marched me back over to the toilet so I could take care of business. It was then that I noticed that my stomach was slightly rounded. I was only six weeks pregnant. Should I be showing yet?

"Grayson?" Sam called out from the bedroom.

"Be there in a sec, Da," my mate called out from behind me.

When I was finished, my mate helped me straighten my sleep pants that I didn't remember putting on and flushed the toilet for me while I washed my hands. He then took my shoulders and directed me back to the bedroom. It felt a little like he was marching me somewhere or that I was in trouble for something.

"Good morning, Jai. I have your tea and some crackers. Edison said you should be able to keep both down."

"Yeah, well, he jumped the gun and got out of bed. He's already been sick," Grayson said with a mock glare. The love I was getting through our bond let me know he wasn't really upset.

"I don't really remember much of yesterday, or this entire last week, really." I crawled into the super-soft bed and sighed as my attentive mate tucked me back in and gave my forehead a quick kiss.

"I'm going to go downstairs and grab some breakfast really quick. I'll be right back, and we can talk, alright?" Grayson asked as he fussed over me.

"Yeah, sure."

"Da will stay with you, and I'll only be gone for a few minutes."

"Grayson, it's okay. Go. Eat. Talk to the other alphas. I can tell something's up. You're agitated," I said to my mate.

"Sorry, sweetheart. I'm trying not to be. There's been a lot going on."

"I know. And you need to go eat. I'll be fine. Sam can sit and tell me all about you as a young cub." My mate groaned at that, and Sam and I both chuckled. But, my mate's omega father just smiled and nodded at me, letting me know he was more than willing to tell me all about my alpha as a young cub. I took a deep breath to garner enough encouragement to drink the tea Edison swore would help with the sickness. And it had so far. But it was certainly nasty smelling and didn't taste overly pleasant. The crackers helped change the taste on my tongue, and for that, I was thankful.

"Okay, I'll be back in just a few," Grayson said as he grabbed a shirt and pulled it on. He picked up his shoes and socks by the door and then he was gone. I looked at Sam who was watching his son leave, but then turned back towards me.

"You make him happy. And he's trying so hard. He feels terrible about this week and what happened to you."

"It's not his fault. I don't understand why he didn't call and ask for help, but I'm glad he finally did."

"He said you asked him not to."

"I did? I don't remember that. I remember him telling me we needed food, and he'd gone several days without eating because he was too worried to leave my side to cook. He should have called someone though."

"That's probably our fault. That's how…he's going to struggle with how things should be done. Just give him time, and he'll figure things out. My mate is difficult, and Grayson has grown up seeing how Ivan handles things. For the most part, he knows that things are actually done differently. He's just never had the experience of seeing how they're done. He needs to see and he'll learn."

"I'm not upset, Sam. I love Grayson. So much. I know he's doing the best he can. I also realize he's still learning. But I know that Ryker, Troy, Wallace, and War will help him. He knows it, too."

"Good. I just want him to be happy. I want him to have more than his father and I do." Sam looked so sad when he talked about his mate. They hadn't been mated very long, had they?

"Sam?"

"Yeah? Everything okay? Do you need Grayson?"

"No, he's in the kitchen talking to the other alphas. He's fine and happy, although, a little worried. He's supposed to get me caught up over breakfast. Do you know what's going on?"

"Yes, I do. But if Grayson said he was going to tell you, he will. It'll be better coming from him anyway."

"Is he okay? Is he in danger?"

"You just said he's fine. Calm down or he's going to rush up—"

Too late. Grayson could be heard stomping up the stairs as fast as he could run. He burst into the room and scanned the place, looking for who knows what.

"Grayson, what's wrong?"

"I got that you were distressed. I need to know you're okay. Are you? What's got you upset?"

"That's my fault, son. I was talking to him, and I inadvertently upset him. I honestly didn't mean to."

I felt bad for Sam; he really was upset that he'd caused me distress. "Sam, don't worry about it. I can't help but be concerned about Grayson. He's my mate and I don't want anything to happen to him. I can sense the tension in the house, anyone could. But you didn't do anything wrong, so please don't feel that you did." I reached for my mate's omega father's hand. I really needed to spend a lot of time getting to know Sam better. I think he could really use a friend.

"Thank you, Jai. That means a lot. Grayson, since you're here, I'll leave you two alone. Just let me know when you need me to come back. Aspen is going to stay with Arik today, and Edison put his foot down and told the alphas that they needed to keep their cubs up here. Linus is helping watch them, as is Cassie. Your sister is going to want a cub of her own soon if she keeps hanging out here with all the babies."

"Well, there's six of them. That's still a lot for just Linus and Cassie," Grayson mentioned.

"It is. Even though War wished he would have waited until after everything settled, Orin should be arriving shortly. Edison was going to go get him. He's anxious to play with his nephews, and I think he's wanting to move back home to the den."

"That's good news. I know him being over with Forest has really upset War. But he understood that Orin needed time," I told Grayson and his da. When Troy had met Elliot, Orin knew his one-sided feelings for Troy were never going to amount to anything. He'd wanted to spend time, waiting for their mates, with Troy's *company*. But Troy had learned his lesson when he was younger. He'd had such an arrangement with Sam and was left all alone when Ivan came through and claimed Sam as his mate. Orin couldn't stay in the den and watch Troy with Elliot so he left. Forest, the Timber Valley Pack Alpha, offered Orin a place to stay and told War he'd keep an eye on his brother. It seemed to work out pretty well for everyone involved. That was over a year ago, and I was glad that Orin was finally ready to come home.

"I'll be back in just a bit. You two enjoy your time together. Grayson, did you eat? You weren't gone long."

"I ate some. I can get something later."

"I'll bring you a tray. Jai, do you want some more tea or crackers?"

When I looked down at the tray across my lap, it was then that I realized I'd drank all of the tea as well as ate all of the white squares that'd become a favorite of mine.

"Actually, water would be good and maybe some more crackers if it's not a bother."

"Jai, you'd never be a bother. Anyway, I offered. I'll have them back up here in just a bit. You two relax and talk. Talking is very important in any relationship."

"Thanks, Da."

Sam nodded and quietly closed the door behind him after he'd stepped through it.

"Grayson, I feel so bad for Sam. He seems sad about the way Ivan is."

"It's been tough on him, I know. But they've only been mated for fifty years. I hope that being around Alpha War and the others, my Dad will realize that things are different from what he thought, and he figures out how to treat Da. In a way, there's always pairings like those that seem so unfair. I mean, Da and Dad are fated, but they're not very happy. Da does his best to make the most of it, and he's tried so hard to get Dad to see that things aren't done here the way his den did them. And losing my brothers and sister when we were attacked, Da took it hard. But so did Dad, and he's actually made an effort and has changed some, just not enough."

"Wow, I guess I didn't realize he used to be worse. You want to tell me what's going on though? I can feel the tension in the air in the house. What's happening?"

"It's Hank and his crew. I refuse to call them a den. No noble alpha would do what he's doing, nor would a den follow along. They're here. Edison has said they'll attack today at some point. That's all he knows. He only gets parts and snippets, but he can't see everything, never could. But he knows that Hank arrives and attacks the same day that Orin does. Oh, and the same day that fate finds another match. That's all he said."

"What? Someone's going to find their mate today? Oh, it can't be someone from Hank's group. They've gone around murdering shifters for no reason other than they are male omegas or have a male mate."

"I know, sweetheart. I'd like to think that fate wouldn't be so cruel, but I just don't know anymore." Grayson ran his fingers through my hair and gave me a gentle, lingering kiss. It stirred something in me, and I was surprised because I hadn't felt anything but terrible for so long. "I need you to know that I love you, and I'll always cherish every moment we're given."

"Grayson, don't talk like that. You're making it sound like I'm going to lose you today. Don't say that." My eyes instantly flooded. That too, was a new thing that I had my pregnancy to thank for.

"I don't plan on going anywhere. But if anything, I've learned that we just never know what fate has in store for us. I never thought I'd lose my two older brothers or sister, but I did. Hank and his group attacked without any regard for anyone. My sister had just given birth to her third cub. When we were far enough away, Dad hid us in a snow den, and him and Mr. Gamble went back to look at the village. I was left with Da, Cassie, Mrs. Gamble, and their son. We found Linus and his parents along the way. They had been running for a while, and we were more than willing to let them travel with us. Anyway, when Dad came back, he said it was one of the most horrific scenes he'd ever seen. And it changed him. He's a little harder, and I know he's angry. I just hope that when Hank attacks, Dad keeps it together enough to not make mistakes. It would kill Da if he lost Dad, too. He's already lost so much."

I wrapped my arms around my mate and just bawled. I cried for Grayson, his parents, and everyone else that had been affected by the monster that was Hank. I dozed off, safe, warm, and loved in my mate's arms.

Grayson — 15

It was so very difficult to leave my sleeping, pregnant mate, but I had no choice. An attack was coming and we knew it. I may have been young, but I was an alpha, and my bear was a force to be reckoned with. I joined Dad and the rest of the alphas downstairs in War's office.

"Who's staying with the omegas? I understand they're not helpless, but two of them are newly pregnant and are experiencing morning sickness," Troy asked.

"Arin has volunteered to stay with them and watch over the cubs and them. Tom and Gloria, Linus' parents, have also agreed to stay with them." Ryker replied.

We all nodded our agreement. Although they were super sweet, as arctic foxes, their shifter halves were small and weren't going to be much of a help in this type of situation. And they wouldn't be able to fight as humans. There was no way Hank was going to attack as his human half. He didn't before. It's not his way.

"Okay, Edison said we have less than an hour before they are on the grounds, so my plan was to shift now and meet them out in the woods. We know this area better than they do. And if at all possible, I want to keep them as far away from the house as possible. I don't want to take any chances with our mates or cubs," War stated. We all were in agreement and immediately started removing our clothing to shift.

"Sweetheart, I love you," I whispered through our bond. I knew Arin would wake him up if things got out of hand. But Jai needed as much rest as he could get, and I didn't want to disturb him. It was difficult to leave him, knowing there was a chance I wouldn't come back, but we needed to do this, and I agreed with War. The farther we were away from the house, the better.

"Edison, do you know how many are in Hank's group?" I asked, curious. I couldn't remember having an answer to that yet, or if it was even asked.

"They have the advantage in numbers, but we have the advantage with Elliot and me."

"I can't thank you two enough. I know this will affect you. But I thought it best if Forest and his group stayed in Timber Valley in case some of Hank's group got away and headed that direction."

"It's okay, War. It will only drain us if we use our powers to strike others down first. Once they come at us, we'll be just fine," Edison told our Alpha.

"If you're sure. I remember what happened with Arianna."

"Yes, but that was different. Is everyone ready? If you are, I'll take you to him. We'll stay in human form first and see if he's willing to talk. It's doubtful, but we have to try," Edison said. When we all nodded, we were gone and then out in the woods. This was it. Dad gave me a surprising hug and looked me in the eyes.

"I'm proud of you, Grayson. You're becoming an amazing young man. I love you, son. Don't think that I don't."

"Love you, too, Dad. Don't go doing something stupid. I know you want revenge for what he did to our family. I do too. But we have to be smarter than him."

"I agree. We need—"

"There they are!" Someone shouted.

Dad and I turned, and when we realized that they weren't going to stop their charge, we all shifted as fast as we could and then the woods were filled with loud growls of fury, followed by ones of pain as the battle started. Until Harvey, I'd never had to fight another shifter in bear form, but it wasn't any easier this time. I knew this was necessary, but it hurt to have to take another's life.

When a massive bear came at me, I swiped out with my own claws and hit him on the snout. Neither of us stopped until we were both winded and bleeding from several wounds that were healing as fast as our bodies allowed. I got my break when the other bear looked in the direction of another that bellowed in pain. I was able to get a deadly swipe of my claws across his neck and in minutes, he was on the ground, dead.

I looked out to our group and noticed that Dad and Troy were both going at who I was sure was Hank. I saw red when Hank got a good swipe in on Dad and he went down. I roared and charged, and within a dozen steps, I collided with the much larger body of the older alpha. My attack gave Troy enough of an advantage to get Hank pinned beneath him and Dad enough time to get his feet back below him. The three of us descended on Hank, Troy allowing Dad to deliver the ending blow for the retribution that he, our family, and the rest of our den needed.

We bellowed our victory, and when I looked up at our group, I realized we were missing Edison. A few others were still battling their opponents. Ryker's Kodiak bear was massive, even larger than the polar bears, and that was saying something. Then I noticed that Ryker was even larger than War, and for some reason I found that fascinating.

When everyone stopped and looked up and around, what I saw made my heart hurt. We were all experiencing heartbreak. So much unnecessary destruction, all because of a deranged alpha with unacceptable beliefs. I shifted back once War had and noticed the wounds even more.

"Gage, are you okay?" War shouted as he ran over to his deputy. Gage had a large gash across his stomach and, like mine several weeks ago, it wasn't healing on its own as it was just too deep. "Edison!"

"He's not here, War. Let me," Elliot said as he rushed to their side. The rest of us were on alert, watching for any threat around. I watched in fascination as Gage's stomach started to heal. He just needed a little help and then his shifter healing took over.

"What do you mean, he's not here? Where's your papa?"

"I guess Hank was expecting us to meet him in the woods. He had two of his men hiding near the alpha house, and once we all left, they snuck in and attacked," Elliot said sadly.

"What!" Several of us shouted.

"Sweetheart? Please, tell me you're okay."

"Oh, thank fates, Grayson. I'm okay, but are you? I need you. Oh, my fates, it's bad."

"Elliot, can you get us all back to the house? What's going on?"

"Yes, I can. Just give me a moment."

Elliot's and my idea of a moment were obviously different since we were in the back yard in the next blink. Without thought, I was racing into the house and to my mate.

"Jai! Where are you?" I shouted just as soon as I was through the door. He came running down the stairs and flung himself into my arms, sobbing. "Shh, I've got you. Please, Jai, where's everyone?"

"Upstairs."

The others hurried past me, and I followed up the rear. Ryker, War, and Troy were all rushing to their mates and cubs. I noticed that Orin was standing with his arm around Aspen's shoulders, and they both looked incredibly sad. I took Jai into our room and closed the door. After sitting down on the bed, I just held my mate. I needed to feel his body next to mine, and I needed to hear the heartbeat of our cub growing in his body. He was my entire world, and I thanked fate that he'd been given to me.

"Jai, I love you. So much."

"Love you too, Grayson. Please, hold me tight. Need to be close to you right now."

"I'm right here, sweetheart, and I'm not going anywhere." I moved us up onto the bed and laid down with Jai curled up half on me, half on the bed. I tugged at the blanket until I had it folded over on us. I was still naked after my shift and was in desperate need of a shower to wash my own dried blood off of me, but right now, I needed to hold my mate some more.

"Arin had woken me up and had me come and stay with Arik and Orin before he went back to the nursery with Sam, Linus, Aspen, Cassie, and the cubs. Arik, Orin and I were sitting and talking and then all of a sudden, we heard a scream. Orin went to the door, ready to shift if he needed. Arin was already on his way down the stairs but stopped when we could just barely see his head on the stairway. He went the rest of the way down and then we heard him talking to Edison. Two of Hank's followers had waited outside for you to leave, then broke into the house. They attacked and killed Tom and Gloria while they were downstairs watching out for us. Why would they be downstairs? Shouldn't they have been up here with us?"

My heart hurt for what had happened. So much death simply because one alpha was so very narrow-minded. I noticed that Jai's breathing started to become labored, and he was becoming more and more agitated. I quickly got up and went to the door to get help.

"Edison! Elliot! Someone!" Edison appeared immediately and rushed past me and into the room. "I'm sorry. He's really getting upset, and I'm worried about him and the baby."

"He's going to be okay. He's understandably upset and he's hyperventilating," Edison told me as he checked on a now sleeping Jai.

"Umm, is he okay?"

"Yes, I helped calm him down a bit. He'll sleep for at least an hour. That will give you plenty of time to take a long shower and get cleaned up. We've got a lot that we're going to have to do around here the next couple days. You two will be welcome to head back to your cabin when Jai is feeling up to it, but I'd feel better if you kept him here for a couple more days. He needs a lot of rest. His body is busy working overtime. Creating life is a beautiful thing, but it is also taxing on the body. He's still recovering from earlier in the week, but he'll be as good as new in a couple more days. Just make sure he keeps drinking his tea. It'll help keep his stomach calm, and he'll be able to keep down foods."

"Thanks for everything, Edison."

"You're welcome, Grayson. That's what family is for. By the way, your parents said to tell you that they'll see you tomorrow. They're in their room and if the sounds coming from it are any indication—"

I groaned at the thought of my parents going at it. We were shifters and sex was a natural thing. But I was almost positive that they didn't have sex anymore. "I didn't need to know that, Edison. I really didn't."

"Yeah, Cassie said the same thing. She ran off with Aspen and Orin."

"Is she okay? Is everyone else?"

"Gage is hurt, but you know that. He's recovering in a room. He's going to be just fine. Ryker's trying to come to terms with his parent's death, as is Linus."

"Wait, Ryker's parents? But we just saw them last night."

"Yes. They were unknowingly attacked by the two that got to Tom and Gloria. I knew we would suffer losses, but not who or how many. There's only so much that the fates let me know. And even then, I'm not allowed to interfere in most cases."

"Edison, are you okay? I'm sure this has all been difficult on you."

"Thank you, Grayson. I'm just fine. Wallace will take care of me later. But for now, I need to see to everyone else."

"Be sure to take care of you, too."

"That's good advice. Where did you ever hear that?" Edison asked with a knowing smile. I looked over at my sleeping mate and fell in love all over again.

"My beautiful mate. He's full of good advice. I'm very blessed to have him."

"I'm glad you feel that way. Take a shower and get cleaned up. We'll have dinner for everyone later if anyone is hungry. You *will* eat though. You suffered more wounds, and your body is still recovering from not having fed it enough this past week."

"Yes, Edison," I said as I smiled at him before I walked off to the shower to wash away the filth and stench of the battle.

Jai — 16

We spent the next three days at War's before finally returning home. My mate, my alpha, was still distant though. He was absolutely perfect in every way, but he seemed distant. I was feeling so much better after a week of regularly drinking the tea that Edison given me and being able to keep down food and water. So I left our bed—I was more than ready to be out of the thing—and went to search for my mate. I found him downstairs on the back deck.

"Hey, what are you doing out of bed?" Grayson asked, but he opened his arms for me anyway. I curled up on his lap, and he immediately wrapped his arms around me.

"Well, I woke up all alone and decided to come search for my mate. So, here I am. Are you okay? You've been distant since everything that happened."

"Yeah, I'm okay. It's just a lot to process. How are you feeling? Your stomach okay? Do you want me to get you some more tea?" I cut off Grayson's rapid-fire questions by pulling his head down so I could reach his lips. It had been so long since I'd kissed my mate that I was determined to change that starting now. When our lips touched, it was almost as sweet and wonderful as it was the first time we'd ever kissed

I maneuvered enough so that I was straddling Grayson's lap on the hanging daybed that we both seemed to prefer. When I thrust my tongue into my mate's mouth, he opened for me and grabbed my ass and pulled my body tightly to his. I could feel his hardness through his jeans and I was positive he was painfully uncomfortable at this point.

"Jai, please tell me you're feeling okay."

"If you don't knot me in the next ten minutes, I'll figure something out to make you pay. Grayson, it's been too long. I need your knot, alpha. Make me scream."

Our clothes were gone almost instantly, and then I was flipped onto my stomach and Grayson was behind me, licking and sucking at my hole. When he thrust his tongue in, my neglected cock spasmed, and I knew I wasn't going to last. "Grayson, gonna cum. Need more."

"No! Mine!" I was flipped back over, and when Grayson swallowed my cock down his throat, he shoved four fingers into my slick channel and rubbed that wonderful spot. I was done and shouted as I emptied down my mate's throat.

"Jai, sweetheart. You okay? I'm sorry. I didn't mean—"

"Don't you apologize. Now pound that knot into me. I need it and I want it hard, deep, and rough. You know exactly how I like it, now give it to me," I shouted as I rolled over. Grayson held my shoulders down while he spread my legs open and then in one quick thrust, he was finally filling my channel again.

"Yes! Harder. Faster. Deeper!" I shouted and my wonderful mate complied. He pounded me until he was panting and dripping with sweat. He'd held his knot back as long as he could, but with a roar, I felt it inflate faster than ever and then he was biting my shoulder and filling me with his hot seed. I exploded below me when he bit me and groaned.

"Grayson!"

When he finally pulled his canines out of my shoulder and licked the wound clean, I started giggling. I simply couldn't help myself.

"Was I that lacking?"

"Fuck, no! I needed that. And since I can feel your cock still spurting inside me, you needed it, too."

"I always need you, mate. You're my everything." Grayson gently rolled us to our sides, and I moaned when I felt his cock twitch again. His knot was perfectly placed and kept hitting my prostate which continually caused tiny orgasms for me.

"Can we do this every day? And you have to add that biting. That was so hot. You need to bite me more."

"I don't want to hurt you, sweetheart."

"Trust me, it didn't hurt. It felt so good. And before you ask, no, you weren't too rough. I feel amazing and it's all because—"

"Yoo-hoo! Jai! Are you two finished yet?"

"Fuck!" I shouted and tried to pull away from Grayson, but I yelped when his knot yanked on my hole. His arms cinched around me, and he held me tight to his body while he growled low and menacing in his chest. "Shh, it's my bà. What's he doing here? My parents live in California."

"What do you mean, it's your bà?" Grayson asked just as my parents came trudging up the stairs of the deck.

"Oh, there you two are. I see that we've caught you at a bad time. Why don't we just go inside and wait for you to become unstuck, and we can meet our new son," my omega father said.

"What the actual fuck?" Grayson roared. I just started laughing; I simply couldn't help it. I was finally feeling better after weeks of being sick, and the first time I got my mate to knot me, my parents showed up out of the blue and caught us knotted together on my back deck. Yep, the fates could be cruel at times.

"Love, I don't think the young alpha is happy with us showing up like this," Bàba said.

"You'd be correct. Now, if you two would mind leaving, I'd appreciate it." Grayson was doing everything he could to shield me from my parents, but there wasn't much he could do while knotted to me.

I simply couldn't stop laughing though. Thankfully, my bàba took mercy on us and pulled my bà into the house behind him. Bàba gave Grayson a sympathetic look and shut the door behind them. Bà never once stopped talking the entire way into the house. Grayson groaned behind me and rolled over onto his back, pulling me on top of his body. My weight pushed his knot a little deeper into my body, and I moaned when my cock started to harden again.

"Fuck!" Grayson said as he wrapped his hand around my cock and started stroking in rhythm to the gentle thrusts as he pushed his hips up into my body. His knot was so large there was no give whatsoever, but I felt the pressure as his cock continually released its seed into my already swollen channel. It was going to be incredibly messy when we finally broke free from each other. "Never going to unknot you if you keep this up, sweetheart."

I moaned again and started to whimper as I got closer to the orgasm I was chasing. "Please, Grayson. Need to cum again."

My mate increased his strokes on my cock, and when my cock exploded for the third time, he caught my release with his other hand and then brought it up to his mouth and licked his hand clean.

"I can't get enough of you, Jai. Never enough." I was completely exhausted, and my body completely relaxed on top of my mate's. He ran his hands gently up and down my body, stopping long enough to tweak my sensitive nipples.

"Gray. Enough. I'll never stop squeezing your knot if you don't stop."

I heard his deep chuckle in response and then his hands were gone from my nipples and were rubbing my baby bump. I sighed contentedly. I was knotted to my mate and carrying his baby. What more could I ask for? Oh yeah, for my parents to not show up unannounced.

"Do your parents always just show up?"

"No. They've never done anything like this before. I talk to my bà weekly and…" I groaned when I realized why they were here. I hadn't called bà in several weeks. I'd been too sick, and it had been the last thing on my mind.

"What?"

"I stopped calling. That's why they're here. Where's my phone? I bet I have a ton of missed calls and texts."

"Well, your phone is inside on your nightstand. I can't exactly go get it for you at the moment," my mate teased. I elbowed him and he immediately stopped laughing.

"Hey, I remember someone being ticklish so you'd better watch it," Grayson said as he ran his fingers gently up and down my ribs.

"No, okay, sorry. Now is not the time for us to get in a tickling match. Do you think you can pull free yet?"

"Not without hurting you, no. And I'm not hurting you, so don't even think about it."

"Okay, so what makes your knot go down faster?"

"I'm not sure. I know a lot of alphas say their knots go down faster when their mates aren't in heat and when they aren't in the second trimester of…"

Grayson and I groaned in unison. I was seven weeks into a five-month pregnancy. I was in my second trimester. No wonder I was so horny.

"Why did I have to meet your parents for the very first time when I was knotted to their son?" Grayson asked.

"You do realize that not only did you meet my parents for the very first time while knotted to me, but also that it's very likely that they heard the whole thing? They heard me begging for you to pound me harder and deeper and everything else that I shouted. They heard your grunts and your roar just before you bit me and my responding roar. Yep, they sure did. How's that make you feel?"

"Are you trying to make me never want to have sex again?" Grayson asked as he gently rolled us and then pulled free. There was still a slight tug, but it didn't hurt and now we were free. I felt a gush of slick and seed and then Grayson moaned before he was once again between my legs and lapping at our combined mess that was leaking out of my body. I moaned at the feeling of his soft tongue as it ran over my used hole. It felt so good.

"Grayson?"

"I know, sweetheart. But your parents are here, I can't knot you again right now."

I let my frustrations be heard, but after my mate pulled away from me and rolled me onto my back, he smiled down at me.

"I promise, I'll take care of you again in the shower. But I can't knot you again until tonight. And trust me, I'm looking forward to knotting you again. Come on, let's pull our pants on, and we'll go shower before you properly introduce me to my new in-laws."

Grayson didn't give me any choice. He got up off of the daybed and tossed my sweats at me and pulled up his jeans. He reached down and grabbed our shirts, then turned and raised an eyebrow at me as I just laid there, stroking my half-hard cock.

"Hey, if you want me to knot you that bad again, I'm all for it. But let's do it inside this time. I really don't relish the thought of your parents coming outside to watch me pound your ass with my dick again."

"That was the incentive I needed." I got up and quickly pulled on my sweats and then followed Grayson into the house. We walked right past my parents to the stairs and up to our room.

Grayson slammed and locked the door before he swung me up into his arms and carried me into the bathroom. He'd promised he'd take care of me in the shower and he did. He pounded me against the shower wall, and I painted the tiles with my release as my mate pulled out and sprayed my hole and back with his.

I was really starting to wonder how adventurous my alpha was. Now wasn't really the time to explore that, or even ask, but I was certainly going to bring it up just as soon as my parents left.

We left the shower, got dressed, and went to join my parents in our kitchen. Bà had made himself at home and Bàba looked both amused as well as uncomfortable.

"Grayson, it's good to finally meet you. I've heard so much about you from my son and my mate," Bàba said as he extended his hand.

"It's good to meet you, too. I just wish it was under different circumstances."

"I apologize. We've called several times but didn't get a response."

"That's my fault, Bà. I've been sick and this past week things have been incredibly rough here." I wrapped myself around Grayson, and like always, he seemed to know what I needed. He gently kissed my temple.

"I love you, Jai. We can tell them later if you'd like. We don't have to do this now."

"Later is good. Thank you for being so understanding."

"With you, anything."

My parents smiled at us, and I knew they understood that Grayson and I were communicating with each other through our bond. My biggest question was, how long were they planning on staying?

Grayson — 17

Jai's parents had to return to California a couple days after they showed up unexpectedly. An, Jai's alpha father, could only get a few days off on such short notice, so they took a long weekend. That was five weeks ago, and I'd spent every spare moment we had knotted to my mate. But now that I was back at work every day while Jai was home, I was distracted and wanted to be at home with my pregnant mate.

"Okay, Grayson. What's troubling you? You've been moaning for the past half hour, and you've been sulking for several weeks now." Troy asked. I realized I was still staring at the same screen I'd opened over an hour ago.

"Sorry, Troy. I'm just distracted. When An and Jing were here, we had a wonderful visit, even if my introduction to my in-laws was a little embarrassing. They're looking forward to coming back, once the baby is born. Not to mention that I can't stop thinking about our visit to Arik this evening. I'm more than a little excited about the prospect of seeing our little cub."

"I remember that. Although, we knew from the get-go that Elliot was carrying triplets, but that didn't detract from actually seeing them and hearing the heartbeats on the monitor. You two will obviously be having a cub, but do you have any idea what you're having? Or is that a warlock thing?"

"I think it's a warlock thing? I'm just excited about the baby and will be happy as long as the baby and Jai are both healthy and fine. That first trimester with the morning sickness was brutal. And why is it morning sickness? Why not pregnancy sickness?"

Troy laughed and then Ryker was poking his head out of his office. He'd been upset about what happened to his parents, but like he'd said, they'd stopped being his parents a long time ago.

"Alright, you two. You're not working, so what's going on?" Ryker asked as he left his office and joined us in the outer room.

"Young Grayson is having difficulties focusing. They're having their ultrasound this evening, and his mind is elsewhere."

"Oh, I remember our first ultrasound. Seeing Edwin for the first time, it was surreal, and I'll admit, I cried when I heard his little heart swish through the monitor."

"Thanks for the warning. I'm sure I'm going to bawl," I said before looking back at my monitor and trying to focus.

"Hey, what else is bothering you?"

"Nothing. Just doing a lot of thinking. And Jing is hinting that he wants to come back and visit again. Soon. I'm trying, but the last time they were here, Jai pulled away from me. Which really was terrible because he had just started his second trimester and I could sense how much he needed…things."

Ryker and Troy both laughed outright. I wished a hole would open up and swallow me and save me from having to talk to my coworkers about this. Maybe my da was a better choice.

"Never mind. I'm going out on patrol or something."

They immediately sobered and got serious.

"Grayson, sit down. We're sorry. I think I can help you a little more with this. Not really, but maybe a little. When Arin was pregnant with Edwin, and we discovered that Aspen needed out of Alaska, we brought him back home with us. And instead of having him stay at War's place, I suggested he stay with us in our cabin. You'd better believe my little mate denied me. He himself suffered for it, too. Warlocks are a little different than shifters, and they sense the aura of those around them. Well, when they find their One, they feel a gentle hum in their bodies. It intensifies until they are claimed. Then, they always feel that gentle hum of their One's aura. Troy and I feel the hum through our mate marks that we were imprinted with when we claimed our mates."

"So you two feel something in those marks on your chests?"

"Yes. It matches what our mates feel in their bodies, but in their bite marks especially," Troy added.

"That's really neat, but what does that have to do with Jai being horny, but not willing to have sex?"

"I was getting there. So anyway, when warlocks go through their second trimester, it's a lot like their fertile period. Only it lasts the entire second trimester. And if they don't get what they need from their mate, the vibrations they feel increase. And it can get incredibly painful. Troy and I feel it in one spot, our mate mark. Arin and Elliot feel it throughout their entire bodies. And when I suggested Aspen stay with us, Arin went to sleep without. All because he didn't want our houseguest to hear us. We were still newly mated, so maybe that's why Jai pulled away. Maybe he was uncomfortable with his parents hearing you two have sex. Especially after what they walked up on. I mean, you two were having sex on the back deck, so you should have been prepared for anyone to show up or hear you."

"True, but we thought his parents were in California. And they heard the whole thing, and I won't mention what we were shouting to each other. And they just walked on up onto the deck and stared down at us. While we were knotted together!"

"Yeah, that'd make me uncomfortable, too."

"You don't say? Yeah, we were both uncomfortable. But he attacked me again in the shower upstairs. But then nothing. They were here for three days, and I could sense his need, but nothing.

And when I asked, he said no, he wasn't feeling well. I didn't get a sense of him not feeling well, but he said it."

"And after they left?"

"After they'd gone back to California, let's just say we spend a lot of time in bed."

"Sounds about right," Troy said. Ryker nodded his head in agreement.

"Grayson, do you know when you'll be home?"

"In a few hours, why?"

"Only because I've just woken up from a nap, and I really could use your knot. You didn't knot me this morning before you left for work. Now I'm really needy for it."

"I'll be home as soon as I can. I'm finishing up paperwork. I'm sorry, sweetheart."

"No, it's okay. I'll be in the bedroom. Please come to me when you get here."

"Always."

"Love you," Jai said and then I heard a moan. Was he?

"Jai? Are you—"

"Grayson...focus."

"What? Huh? Oh, sorry. I was just...distracted." They didn't need to know that my mate was at home misbehaving. He was going to...

"Grayson!" Troy and Ryker said at the same time.

"Sorry. Okay, what?"

"Yes, we understand it's difficult. But we need you to focus."

"So if Jai's parents come back, you're thinking he's going to lose interest again?"

"Basically, yes. And I'm rather enjoying this part of the pregnancy."

"Trust us, every shifter enjoys this part of the pregnancy," Troy told me while shaking his head.

"Okay, so what do I do? How do I keep my in-laws in California?"

"That seems pretty simple. Just have Jai tell them to wait until closer to when the baby is due," Ryker told me.

"Okay, but how do I get Jai to agree?"

"Right now, I'd imagine that if you remind him while you're having sex, or right after, would be the most successful way. If he remembers what you two just did, he'll likely be willing to take the step needed to keep his omega father in California until he's further along," Ryker suggested.

"Do you think that'll work?"

"Honestly, I think it's worth a try. And you've got nothing to lose except houseguests that keep you and your mate apart when you both need to be together as much as possible."

"Thanks, Ryker. I really appreciate it. I'll bring it up to Jai this evening when I get home."

"Yeah, speaking of that, why don't you head on home? There's not a whole lot to do. With it getting dark so early, and the parks closed because of snow, there's really not a whole lot to do around here right now."

"You sure?"

"Yeah, absolutely. I was going to tell you and Troy to go home anyway."

"You don't have to tell me twice," Troy said moments before he was gone.

"I guess he called for a ride?"

"Yes, it's convenient for sure."

"I'll take your word for it. I appreciate you talking to me, Ryker. I've had so many questions and you and the other alphas have been great about answering them. I really do appreciate it. Some things just didn't get discussed when I was growing up and it leaves some uncertainty now."

"How are your parents?"

"It's a little odd that my da is pregnant the same time that my own mate is, but it's not uncommon. I mean, Cassie was born after my parents' first grandchild was born so it's nothing new. It's just different when it's your mate and everything."

"That's understandable. But I'm sure that Ivan and Sam are happy about the pregnancy. I've only seen them once since the whole Hank thing."

"It's strange. My dad is doting on da. I can't remember him ever having done that before. I'm not complaining, but it's just so out of character."

"Well, Ivan went through a lot over the last year and a half. And he lost his first three cubs, their mates, and all of their cubs when Hank attacked. This pregnancy probably surprised him a little, but also gave him a sense of renewed hope. Maybe it'll be what your parents needed to finally connect how they should have in the beginning. I know that Ivan has been spending a lot of time with War."

"Yeah, I hope, for Da's sake, he actually listens when War has some advice for him."

"It would appear he is. Now, turn off your computer and head on home to your mate. I'm sure he'd be excited for you to show up so early."

"Yes, he would," I said as I saved my document and shut down my computer. I grabbed my phone off of the desk and then my coat off the back of my chair. Ryker was standing at the door ready to lock up by the time I was ready.

"Have a good night, Ryker."

"Thanks. You too, Grayson." Ryker said before he vanished just as Troy had. Yep, I agreed, it was convenient because he and Troy were already home with their mates, and I still had to drive to mine. I didn't mind though. It would be nice to surprise Jai. We had more than enough time to spend the afternoon knotted together before we had to be at Arik's office for our ultrasound.

I got into my old pickup and started it up. After carefully backing out of my space, I headed in the direction of the cabin I shared with my mate. There was snow on the ground, but it was December in Montana. There was supposed to be snow on the ground.

Maybe I could get my mate to go outside and play in the snow later. The first time we'd shifted in front of each other there'd been snow on the ground. I thought back to that day and remembered all of the enjoyment we'd both gotten.

When I got home, I pushed the button on my visor and opened my garage door and pulled in. My mate met me at the bottom of the stairs, and when I picked him up, he squealed as I carried him up the stairs.

"How long are you home for?"

"Until tomorrow. Ryker sent us home. Work was slow and boring."

"It often is in the winter. Since you have enough time, will you knot me?"

"Sweetheart, I'll always give you my knot. Even if we don't have time, I'll still be willing," I said as I sat my pregnant mate down on our bed so I could strip out of my clothes.

"How do you want me?"

"Whatever's most comfortable for you."

When Jai rolled over and laid down on a pillow, I knew from the position he'd chosen, he wanted it a little rougher than I was comfortable with, but I needed to take care of my mate. He knew what he could and couldn't handle, and if he wanted a marathon of sex, he'd get it.

"Sweetheart, are you sure?"

"Yes. Please, Gray? Once we're knotted, this way is easiest to change positions," Jai said as he wiggled his enticing ass at me.

"Alright. How rough?"

"As rough as you're willing. Arik said it's okay."

I groaned as I slid my cock into his already slick hole. I didn't want foreplay this afternoon, and neither did my mate it seemed.

Jai — 18

"Sweetheart, wake up. Come on, Jai. We have to get in the shower."

"Huh? What? Why? Come back here and snuggle some more." I heard laughter just before the warm body of my mate left the bed. I grabbed his still-warm pillow and pulled it to myself before I snuggled back in for more sleep. I vaguely heard the shower turn on in the bathroom but didn't pay any attention. That was, until my mate pulled the covers off my naked body.

"Hey! It's cold!"

"Yes. It's December. It's supposed to be. But we need to shower. Up you go," Grayson said as he picked me up from our bed.

"But I don't want to shower, I want to snuggle," I replied as I buried my face in my mate's neck. I gave his mating bite a quick kiss. I got the expected moan from above so I smiled.

"Sweetheart, have you forgotten that we have an appointment with Arik at five?" Grayson asked as he stepped into the shower.

He gently set me on my feet under the warm spray and I groaned, it felt so good.

"What? Arik?" Realization hit me and I immediately perked up. "Oh, the baby! I want to see the baby!" I grabbed the bottle of shampoo and started my shower. When I got to my rather large bump, I realized I could barely reach my package anymore.

"Need or want some help there, mate?"

"I'll take it. When did I get so big? I don't remember Arin being this big when he was twelve weeks."

"Arin's a lot taller than you, sweetheart. I think that helped. We can ask Arik if everything's okay. I'm sure it is though. We can both still hear the baby's heartbeat, so don't get worked up over something that's most likely not an issue."

"You're right. I can't help it though. We still have about eight weeks, but do you think you'd want to go shopping this weekend? I'd really like to get some things for the baby. We haven't bought anything yet. Not even diapers."

"Calm down, sweetheart. We have plenty of time, and yes, I'd love to go shopping this weekend. We can put you in your puffy coat, and you should be just fine. I won't be able to take you out to lunch though, sorry."

"I understand. Don't apologize. I haven't really thought much about everything we need to do for the baby."

"We'll take care of it this weekend. Come on, let's get dressed and head over to Arik's. I was told we'd be staying for dinner as well so we won't need to worry about that when we get home."

"We are? That's wonderful. I'd love to chat with everyone and get caught up," I replied as I pulled a shirt over my head. When I tried to pull it down over my protruding belly, it was too snug and wouldn't stay down. Grayson smiled at me and handed me one of his shirts. He wasn't overly large, but he was bigger than me, and his shirt provided a little bit of growth room still, so I saw me helping myself to lots of my mate's shirts in the future.

"Sweetheart, you don't have to stay in the cabin every day. You can come to work if you want, and I'm sure that Arin, Arik, or Elliot wouldn't mind you visiting them. Aspen and Orin, too. They're all at Arik's every day so I don't see why it'd be an issue for you to spend time with them. And if you miss working, I know Ryker wouldn't mind you showing up. But you know there's not a lot going on right now."

"I do. I remember it being so boring in the winter. I really don't regret taking some time off. I've actually thought about that more, and what do you think about me resigning my position? I want to have more cubs with you, and even if we can't, it'll be five years before this one is ready to go to school. I want to be home with him or her until then."

"Jai, you know I'll support you in whatever you decide to do. If you want to resign, that's fine. I'm still nowhere near the paygrade you are, but I also know that we're not hurting because you've saved for so long. I'd like to think that it would have been the same if our roles were reversed. If I was the older of the two, I would've saved and been ready for a mate. I've realized it's just what we do."

"Thank you." I threw my arms around Grayson and squeaked when he picked me up by my ass. He gave me a loud, noisy kiss and then set me back down and grabbed his boots.

"You ready?"

"Yes. This shirt is really comfy," I replied as I rubbed the soft cotton material. I'd definitely claimed Grayson's shirt as mine. Why did it take me so long to realize his shirts were so soft?

"You're more than welcome to my shirts, sweetheart. Now, come on, or we'll be late. And I'll admit, I'm anxious to see and hear our baby."

"Me, too. I wish Arik could have gotten us in earlier, but I understand. How's Sam doing? I haven't talked to him in a few days."

"He seems to be doing okay. He and Dad are over the moon about the baby. Cassie not so much."

"No? Why isn't she happy about the baby?"

"I don't know. I think she's spoiled and used to being the sole center of Da's attention," Grayson said as he backed out of the garage. "After everything that's happened, Da became much more, I don't know, clingy, for lack of another word, with me and Cassie. Then I moved out and found you almost immediately so all he had left was Cassie."

"Yeah, but when he went into heat, didn't she realize that's where babies came from?" I couldn't help it, I was laughing. I probably shouldn't have been because it wasn't a nice thing to do, nor was it the most advisable thing when a baby was determined to push on your bladder, but I really couldn't stop myself.

"I know. You'd think she'd know that since she just turned eighteen. Unfortunately, she's not scented her mate anywhere in the den. I think she had a crush on Gage, but we all know how that turned out."

"Yes, but he's happy. He and Linus needed each other and met at the perfect time. And the difference in him is remarkable."

"It is."

"Grayson, I need to ask you something."

"Sweetheart, you know you can always ask me anything. What is it?"

"I really want to know if we're having a boy or girl. I'd love to decorate the room accordingly, and I want to know if I should buy tons of blue outfits or pink ones."

"Jai, you know I only want a healthy mate and baby. If you want to know if we're having a boy or girl, let Arik know. I don't mind knowing. I'll gladly spend hours shopping with you."

"Thank you," I said as Grayson pulled into the drive at War's house. Arik had a second office set up in the back that he used as an exam room. So far, only our den and two other couples from Forest's pack had needed Arik's services. He was fine with that since he had twins to chase after, and he was pregnant again.

"There you two are. I was beginning to think you'd forgotten," Arik said in greeting at the door.

"No. Jai was napping, though, and didn't want to get up."

"True. The bed was warm and comfortable," I replied as I walked in the door. The smile had left Arik's face though.

"Wow, Jai, you popped. We know when you conceived, but I'd think you were ready to give birth if I didn't."

"I feel ready. Can I use the bathroom before we start?"

"Actually, no. It'll be easier to see the baby if your bladder is full and pushes things forward. Come on though, we can get started right away and then you can go to the bathroom after I take all the measurements. We can finish the rest after."

"Okay. You're right behind me, right? You're eleven weeks?"

"Yes."

"Then why don't you look like you're ready to pop?"

Arik laughed before replying. "Because I'm about six inches taller than you. With Papa's help, I did my ultrasound earlier this morning. Although I didn't need to, I confirmed that we were having a single little tigress this time. War is over the moon. He's so excited to get a little princess. And Papa let us know she's a tiger."

"A girl? Really? And a little tiger at that? Congratulations! I'm so excited for you. I'm sure Harrison will be super protective of his little sister. And of course, even though Bradley is an omega, I'm sure he will, too."

"We can only hope. But knowing my luck, she'll be a huge troublemaker. Okay, up on the table with you," Arik said. I backed up to the table, and before I could even struggle to get on it, my mate was there to lift me on.

"It's handy having alphas around," I said as Grayson looked down at me on the table.

"It can be, surely. Now, before we start, yes or no about knowing the sex?"

"Yes." Grayson and I responded at the same time.

"Alright, then. Let me get the gel and we'll get started."

"Arik, congratulations about the little girl. I have a feeling Jai secretly wants a little girl but won't admit it."

"What? Why would you say that?"

"Sweetheart, I found your list of names. Every last one of them are female names."

"I'm sorry, Grayson. I know you want a son."

"No, sweetheart. I want a healthy baby. And a happy mate. I don't care if we have a boy or a girl. I just want everyone to be healthy." Grayson ran his fingers through my hair in what I'd come to realize was a relaxing gesture for him. He loved to play with my hair, and I'd gotten used to it. I often fell asleep with him knotted inside me and him running his fingers through my hair. I needed to make sure I didn't cut it too short, or he wouldn't be able to do it as often.

"Okay, you two. Let's get started. Jai, I need you to pull your shirt up so I can squirt the gel on your belly."

"Alright," I said as I pulled the front of the shirt up to my chest. That should be enough room, right? Arik squirted the blue goo on my stomach and then picked up a gray thing and then swirled the goo around my stomach with it. He stopped, reached over and pushed several buttons on the keyboard, and then all of a sudden, the room filled with a swishing sound.

"Is that…" I started to ask.

"Yeah, hang on though." Arik was solely focused on the screen and wasn't looking at either of us. He moved the wand and pushed a few more buttons and then we heard more swishing. "So you two know you're having twins, right?" Arik asked as he turned the monitor towards us, and there on the screen were two perfect looking babies.

I burst out in tears, and Grayson wrapped his arms around me tried to soothe me.

"Shh, it's okay, sweetheart. I'm happy. I'm ecstatic. Aren't you? I can't get a good read on your feelings."

"Two, I'm going to be a whale!"

"Jai, stop. You're not going to be a whale. You're beautiful. And you know I can't get enough of you."

That, combined with the several mental images that Grayson sent me stopped my pity party in seconds. I had to concentrate on not getting hard, and I almost succeeded. Almost.

"So, whatever your mate said seemed to work. I'll tell you this, War was crazy about my belly when I was carrying the twins. Same this time around. But back to your two bundles. You're in luck, you get one of each. Baby A, here is a girl, and that's her brother there hiding behind her."

"Why haven't we heard both heartbeats?" Grayson asked. That actually made me worry.

"Because he's behind his sister instead of beside her. That's probably about to change though, because they're running out of room, and they'll shift. Also, here, listen," Arik said as he turned up the volume on the machine. If we listened very closely, we could hear the swish of his heartbeat just a fraction of a second after his sisters. They were so close together we never noticed.

Grayson — 19

Twins. We were having twins. As in two. One of each. A boy and a girl. Both. I was in shock, and it was a good thing. My mate was over the moon, and he could hardly wait to tell everyone. So many things made more sense now. Why he was so sick at the beginning; why he was so much larger than Arik now. Although, Arik being taller than Jai certainly helped. I tried to focus on what Arik and Jai were talking about, but it was no use. My bear was preening at the realization that he'd put not one, but two cubs in our mate's belly.

"Grayson."

"Huh?" I said as I looked from Jai's stomach to his face. "Yeah, sweetheart?"

"I asked if you'd heard what Arik said, but I got my answer. You didn't."

"I'm sorry. What was it you said, Arik?"

"I said congratulations and let Jai know that he'd need to come in and see me each week now. You two should expect to only have about six more weeks, so I hope you're ready."

"No, we're not. But we plan on getting everything this weekend. Now I guess we'll be getting two of everything," I told him. He nodded and then reached over and grabbed a towel and wiped off Jai's stomach.

"You can go pee now, and we'll finish when you're back."

"Perfect," Jai said as he started to sit up. I helped him and he was gone before I could even stand up.

"Well, that explains why he has to pee all the time."

"It does. It also explains why he's so much larger than I expected. That's what threw me off when he entered. I didn't expect him to have popped so much already."

"I didn't think anything of it. My bear knew Jai was pregnant before I did, but he never really indicated anything beyond that. Why didn't Edison say something? He had to have known."

"Yes, Papa would have been able to tell almost immediately. But he's been scolded too many times about spilling things we might not want to know so he's learned to keep quiet."

"Well, that explains that then." Jai came back with a relieved look on his face, and I helped him climb back up on the table.

"Okay, ready to proceed?" Arik asked. I nodded while Jai responded.

"So if I only have about six weeks left, how big am I going to get?"

"Well, you'll get as large as your twins need you to be. Your boy, although behind his sister, I saw him immediately. He's a bit bigger than his sister, which is common so you don't need to worry about anything. Their measurements all check out, their heartrates are where they're supposed to be, although, normally boys have a slower heartrate. I would imagine it's just because he's behind her and fate decided to keep him a secret for now. Let me get a few pictures for you two and then we can go have dinner. Dad made beef stew and homemade biscuits and I can't wait."

"I remember his chicken stew he made when Jai was sick."

"Yeah, that's good, too. But his beef stew is even better."

Arik squirted some more goo on Jai's stomach and then moved the wand around and stopped every so often. He kept pushing buttons on the keyboard which led to the sound of the little printer as it spit out the images of our cubs. Jai and I were both transfixed at the images on the screen, and all too soon, Arik was finished and was wiping my mate's stomach off again.

"Alright, you two. I'll want to see you next week, and we'll talk about what all you can expect. Jai, if your omega father can come out, I'd say have him come no later than three weeks from now. You have six left, but you're not going to feel like doing much of anything those last few weeks. Trust me on that one. Sex, you two are welcome to continue having sex for as long as you're interested, Jai. If it hurts, don't do it. Otherwise, everything is fair game, and you're welcome to it. Do either of you have questions?"

I shook my head no as did Jai. "If I think of any, I'll be sure to give you a call though."

"Sounds good. You both have my number, and Troy or Ryker can always get in touch with me through Arin or Elliot. They're always here during the day with their little ones."

"Sounds good, Arik. Thank you."

"Naw, don't thank me. This is what I do. And I'm excited to deliver your two cubs. But I'm pregnant, and I've heard Jai's stomach growling for the past ten minutes, so let's go eat."

"Sorry. It was the mention of stew. I love stew."

"I don't blame you. I'm hungry, too," Arik replied with a smile on his face. He left his little office, and we followed behind, carrying our strip of black and white photos of our cubs.

"Hey, there's the lucky couple. Do you know what you're having? We're getting a little tigress this time," War beamed.

"See, I told you he was prancing around and was over the moon about it," Arik said and for whatever reason, I found that funny and laughed at the Alpha Mate's obvious teasing of his mate.

"Actually, we're getting one of each," my mate said as he held up the strip for everyone to see. The room erupted in congratulations, hugs for Jai, and back slaps for me. I was so excited, and I couldn't wait to get home and talk to my mate about our cubs. It had hit all of a sudden and I realized just how much we had to do in a short period of time.

Fortunately, for me, by the time we'd finished with dinner, Jai had a written list of each and every baby store we'd need, and if we wanted, we wouldn't even have to leave the house to do any of our shipping. Jai was quiet on the ride home, and it wasn't until I glanced over at him as we'd passed under a street lamp that I noticed he'd dozed off.

He'd still been enthusiastic about everything, but I noticed he'd started slowing down after he'd been up for too long. Not only were his energy levels draining faster, but his pregnant belly was becoming cumbersome. Why didn't we think that he was having multiples before now?

"Hey, sweetheart, we're home. Do you want to walk, or do you need me to carry you?"

It was as if a switch flipped, and my mate was suddenly full of energy. So maybe it was just catnap that provided a little boost in energy.

"Can we check out these sites? We should probably call our parents, too. Oh, and I was thinking, since Sam is pregnant, as well, would it be okay if I asked Bà to come out and stay with us like Arik suggested?"

"Okay, slow down. One thing at a time," I replied with a huge smile on my face. Jai was so adorable when he was this fired up.

"Sorry. I'm overly excited. I can't believe I didn't sense the second baby."

"It's okay, sweetheart. I didn't either. But what matters is that we have two healthy little ones, who are about to join us in a few weeks. Now why don't we go to the den, and I'll start a fire in the fireplace. Curl up on the couch and then I'll grab the tablet, and we can snuggle and shop. After we call our parents, though. You go ahead and call Jing and let him know the good news. And yes, he's welcome to come and stay whenever you'd like. But sweetheart, promise me that you won't pull away this time like you did when they showed up last time."

"I won't. I'm really sorry about that. For whatever reason, I started thinking about what they heard and saw, and I got a little embarrassed. I'm so much more comfortable with us now, it won't be an issue. If they hear me shouting for you to pound me harder, well, they have to understand that you're young and sexy, and I like it when you pound me hard. Besides, when I first told them about you, bà went on and on with how lucky I was that you were younger than me. Your endurance levels were going to make me very happy. He was correct. They do. But more than that, you do. I love it that you're perfectly happy with just snuggling and cuddling on the couch if that's all I'm in the mood for."

"Sweetheart, why would I not be? I'll never force you to do something you don't want to do. Ever. All I want is for you to be happy and healthy. That's it. If I can be the reason you're those things, then I'm good. I feel that I've accomplished something then. Now sit," I said as I stopped in front of the couch. I grabbed the throw and threw it over his lap and leaned down and gave my mate a kiss. "Do you need anything else or want something to drink?"

"No, I'm good. But I do want your company."

"I'll be with you in just a few minutes. Give Jing a call while I start the fire and then get the tablet, and we'll see what kind of damage we can do to the bank account."

"Oh, honey, you have to know by now that I can do serious damage to the bank account."

"Yeah, I do. And the babies need things and we have nothing. Also, it might be wise to set up an auto delivery for diapers and formula. But first, phone calls," I said before I turned and went over to the fireplace to light it. Thankfully, we always kept it clean and prepped for the next fire so all I had to do was light it and wait. Once the fire was going, and I had good-sized logs in it, I replaced the screen and then went up to the bedroom to grab the tablet. I heard Jai talking to his dads when I reentered the den, and when I glanced at my mate, he was smiling with tears of joy in his eyes. I handed him a couple tissues as I walked to him with the tablet.

"Yes, Bà, I promise. Grayson said you're welcome to come and stay any time. Do you need to hear it from him?"

I gave my mate a panicked look when he shoved the phone towards me. I tried to shake my head no, but it was no use, I was going to be stuck talking to Jing. I couldn't tell my mate no so I relented and exchanged the phone for the tablet and sat down behind my mate. He snuggled in between my legs and laid back on my chest.

"Hey, Jing. How are you and An doing?"

"Grayson, you're having twins! As far as I know, our family has never had twins before."

"It's very common for polar bears to have twins. But since we're having a boy and a girl, Jai released two eggs so maybe there's twins there somewhere."

"Yes, maybe...." Jing got quiet, and I knew exactly what he wanted. My mate's parents seemed to think I disliked them for some reason, but that wasn't the case at all. And I knew exactly how I could go about fixing that, as well as making my mate happy.

"Jing, would you and An like to come and visit? I know that Jai would love to have you stay with us for as long as you'd can. I'd love to get to know the both of you better, and it would be a great help with the babies."

The loud squeal in my ear gave me the only answer I needed. I handed the phone back to my mate and scooted down on the couch a little more to get comfortable.

Jai — 20

We were ready and I was over being pregnant. I was as big as a whale, like I anticipated, and I could hardly move. I was ready to hold my babies in my arms instead of having them fighting for room in my too-small stomach. I'd already carried the twins a week longer than Arik had expected, and I was beginning to think they weren't ever going to come out.

It was a race to see who delivered first, me or Arik. The other omegas who were pregnant weren't even in consideration, because if I was still pregnant that far from now, I'd kill my mate. Not really, I could never live without Grayson, but I was more than ready to have these kids.

"Sweetheart, you're distressed. Do you need something?"

"Yes. These kids out of my belly. Now. Make them come out, honey. I hurt, I ache, I can't sleep, I can't get comfortable, and I'm—oh shit!"

"Jai, I'll be right there."

In the middle of my tantrum, my stomach contracted and my water finally broke. I was standing in the middle of the kitchen trying to reach a glass in the cupboard, and then all of a sudden, I felt the wonderful gush of fluid between my legs. Yep, it was wonderful simply because that meant our twins would be born today.

"Here I am, sweetheart. Let's get you to the bedroom. Bà is already fixing it up for the delivery and An is calling Arik to see if he has any suggestions or anything." Grayson swung me up into his arms and carried me swiftly up the stairs to our bedroom. He sat me down on the bed just as another contraction hit. I noticed the pained look on Grayson's face, and it made me question him.

"Grayson, are you feeling the contractions?" I asked as a strong pulling feeling hit me. Was that…

"Grayson, I want you to get behind him on the bed and support him."

"Yes, Bà," Grayson said as he climbed onto our bed behind me like Bà had instructed. He pulled me up against his chest and then my omega father yanked my soaked sweatpants off.

"Jai, your omega line is almost fully open. Just another contraction or two and then we can deliver the babies."

I cringed as another searing pain hit my stomach. It felt as if it was being ripped apart, and in a way, that's exactly what was happening. Bàba came rushing in holding out his phone, a less than calm look on his face.

"Arik's in labor. Edison said Elliot has offered to assist if you'd like."

"Yes!" I shouted just as another contraction hit, and I tried to curl up to make it stop. Seconds later, Elliot appeared and I was relieved. I knew Bà would do a wonderful job, but I wanted someone else there as well.

"Hey, Jai. I hear your two rascals have finally decided to make an appearance. Let's get them delivered, shall we?"

"Thank you, Elliot. Yes, please." He chuckled and Bà moved up to my side and grabbed a washcloth and ran it over my face. When did I start sweating so bad?

"Okay, then. Let's see if we can get you delivered before Arik. Jai, your omega line is now open, so when your next contraction hits, I want you to curl up a little and give a little push for me. I'll get the baby out, but you have to push them up to me, alright?"

"Yep," I grunted as a contraction hit, and I did exactly as Elliot had said and gave a little push when Grayson sat us both up just a bit. He'd made the mistake of lacing his fingers with both of mine, and I squeezed his hands as tightly as I could.

"I promise to never make you go through this again, sweetheart. I'm so sorry."

"Shut it. We're doing this every flippin' year that I go into heat so get ready for a bunch of little pandas and polar bears running around here."

"Congratulations you two, it's a girl, and she's a panda. Grayson, would you like to cut the cord?" Elliot asked as he pulled a slimy, wrinkled baby from my belly. I relaxed back onto Grayson's chest. He leaned forward just a bit, and after shifting a hand, he cut the cord with a simple swipe of his claws. Shortly after, we were met with the beautiful sound of our little panda's wail. "She's got a set of lungs on her, doesn't she?" Elliot asked as he waved his hand and then she was clean and wrapped up in a light purple blanket. "Here you go, grandpa, why don't you hold your little granddaughter while I get your grandson born."

I looked up in time to see Bàba take our daughter from Elliot's arms, and he had tears in his eyes. I'd only ever seen Bàba cry when babies were born. They brought him such great joy and happiness. While my alpha father cooed to our little princess, another contraction hit just as Elliot looked up at me and smirked.

"Well, we half beat him. According to Troy, little miss Valentina was just born. Your little princess beat her by about a minute. One more push, Jai, and we'll have your little guy here to join his sister."

I curled up and gave another push, and then after I felt the increase of pressure in my stomach, it was over, and Elliot was holding up a much larger, yet still slimy baby.

"Congratulations, Daddy. You've got yourself a little polar bear alpha here. You going to cut the cord again, Grayson?"

My mate reached out, and once again, cut the cord. By the time he wrapped his arms around my shoulders tightly, his hand was once again human skin. Grayson buried his face in my neck and let out a loud sob. Through our bond, I felt everything he was going through. When our son let out an equally loud cry, we both looked up at him, and I broke right along with my mate. We were parents. We'd done that. We'd created those two beautiful little ones. Elliot helped my omega line close, and then with just a thought from him, I was cleaned up and was wearing fresh clothes, and there were clean linens on the bed. Grayson was equally clean when I leaned back into him more.

"Here you go, Daddy. What are you two going to name them? Troy's driving me crazy asking." Elliot handed us a little bundle wrapped up in a blue blanket, and I looked down at my son while my mate continued to cry on my shoulder. Grayson started gently rocking us back and forth, and I knew he was going to cry harder when I announced his name.

"We're going to call him Kaiden, after Grayson's brother who was murdered by Hank. And our little princess will be called Li, after Bà's mother." Grayson hugged me tighter before he let out a mournful wail. I knew he grieved for his lost brothers and sister and their mates and cubs. Everything that Hank had taken from them was for no reason at all and would impact them for the rest of their lives.

"I love you so much. So very much, sweetheart. Thank you. For everything. For giving me two perfect, beautiful little cubs, for loving me and not telling me to take a hike when I messed up, for honoring my brother in such a beautiful way. For being my mate and being just as beautiful inside as you are outside."

"I love you, too, Grayson."

When I realized it was incredibly quiet in the room, I looked up and saw that both of my parents and Elliot all had tears running down their cheeks. They all knew what we'd gone through, and they understood the meaning and importance of what Grayson and I had done. My mate had tried to argue with me about little Kaiden's name, but I wasn't having it.

"Is it okay if I let Troy know?"

"Yes, please announce it to everyone. We need to call Ivan and Sam though, so please tell them to not announce it quite everywhere yet," I told Elliot. He smiled knowingly.

"Can do. We'll let you to get acquainted with your new little ones for a bit. If you need anything, just give one of us a call, alright?"

"Yes. Thank you...Elliot," Grayson said brokenly as he ran a finger down our son's cheek. When Elliot and my dads left, I sighed. I had everything I could ever need right here. I had a wonderful mate that I adored and two beautiful cubs with him.

"Would you like to hold him, Grayson?"

"No. He's good where he's at. I just need to hold you right now. I'll hold them both later though. We're going to be so busy. Not as busy as Troy and Elliot, but busy."

"Yeah, and War and Arik have their little girl now. That's three for them."

"I like the name they picked. It's cute," Grayson said. I had to agree. It was cute, but luckily for her, it would be a beautiful name when she was older.

"I wonder where they got the idea?" I asked. I hadn't talked to Arik in a while. I'd been so miserable that I didn't want to talk to anyone, really.

"Sweetheart, it's Valentine's Day. Today is February 14th. I was actually bringing you your gift when your water broke."

"What? I didn't get you anything, Grayson. I didn't even realize."

"Don't worry about it. I'm sure Jing is adding your newest orchid to your sunroom."

"You got me an orchid? What kind?"

"A vanda exotic purple orchid. It reminded me of you when I saw it."

"Really? How?"

"It looked strong and determined. It just screamed, *take me home to your mate*. So, I did. Happy Valentine's Day, mate. I love you."

"I love you too. Call your dads. I'm ready for a nap, but I want to talk to Sam first."

"You sure?"

"Yes. They need to know their grandchildren have arrived."

Grayson pulled out his phone and connected the call but put it on speakerphone. "Hey, Da. You're a grandpa."

"Really? When? Ivan! Jai's had the babies!"

"Just a little bit ago. We have a beautiful little lady named Li, and she has a brother named Kaiden that is a few minutes younger."

We could hear Sam cry through the phone, and it was Ivan that responded to us.

"That's such a beautiful thing, you two. Your brother would be so proud of you, Grayson."

"I'd like to think so. I understand you're not feeling the best, Da, but I'd love it if you two could come by and see the cubs sometime."

"We'd love to, Grayson. Does tomorrow work?" Sam asked. He was the pregnant one, so if tomorrow worked for him, it would work for us.

"Yes, that's great. Come by any time. My parents are still here, and Bà is planning on staying for a few more weeks."

"That sounds wonderful, you two. We know what it's like to be new parents so enjoy your cubs. We'll see you all tomorrow," Ivan said.

"Thanks, Dad. We will. Bye," Grayson said and then they were gone.

"Well, now that that's over, what should we do?" I asked as I looked down at my sleeping cubs.

"Well, should I even suggest putting them in their bassinette? Are you ready to give them up for a nap?"

"Shouldn't we feed them?" I asked.

"They haven't cried for food yet, so maybe not. They'll let us know when they're hungry. Let me put them just right here, and you can lie down and rest."

"I love you, Grayson. Thank you for giving me a chance."

"What are you talking about? It's you who gave me the chance. I was the ass."

"Maybe. But look at us now, we have the two most beautiful cubs."

"I love you too, sweetheart."

Grayson carefully took each of our cubs from my arms and gave them a gentle kiss before placing them in the bassinette and then joining me in bed. It felt so heavenly to have my mate and cubs so close.

The End

Connect with Taylor!

Thank you so much for reading Grayson's Enlightenment. I hope you enjoyed it! Up next in the Honey Creek Den series will be Gage and Linus's story.

Want to know when my next book is being released? How about giveaways and sales?

You can find me on Facebook here:
https://www.facebook.com/profile.php?id=100016810573958

My reader group is here:
https://www.facebook.com/groups/729846413870305

You can find me on Instagram here:
https://www.instagram.com/author_taylor_rylan/

You can find me on Twitter here:
https://twitter.com/TaylorRylan1

You can visit my web page here:
www.taylorrylan.com

All signed paperbacks can be found there in the store.

Join my newsletter here:

http://eepurl.com/dtBOKz

I promise not to spam you or ever sell your email address to anyone. My newsletter will be used solely for marketing and announcements about upcoming releases and sales.

Feel free to contact me! I would love to hear from you.

If you enjoyed this book, please consider leaving a review on Amazon. It doesn't have to be long; any review helps indie authors like me. The more reviews we get, the better chance we have of Amazon promoting our books for us! Thank you!

Current List of Books

Shifters/MPREG
Honey Creek Den Series

War's Mate

https://mybook.to/WarsMate

Troy's Warlock

https://mybook.to/TroysWarlock

Ryker's Enchantment

https://mybook.to/RykersEnchantment

Grayson's Enlightenment

https://mybook.to/GraysonsEnlightenment

Contemporary Series
Men of Crooked Bend Series

My Forever, My Always: Men of Crooked Bend Book 1

https://mybook.to/MFMAebook

My Choice, My Chance: Men of Crooked Bend Book 2

https://mybook.to/MCMCebook

My Survivor, My Savior: Men of Crooked Bend Book 3

https://mybook.to/MSMSebook

My Truth, My Future: Men of Crooked Bend Book 4

https://mybook.to/MTMFebook

My Heat, My Home: Men of Crooked Bend Book 5

https://mybook.to/MHMHebook

My Love, My Valentine: A Men of Crooked Bend Companion Novel (4.5)

https://mybook.to/MLMVebook

Made in the USA
Columbia, SC
01 December 2018